Rebecca

Mail Order Brides of Wichita Falls

CYNDI RAYE

Rebecca

Mail Order Brides of Wichita Falls
Book 6
by
Cyndi Raye

---

1. http://www.CyndiRaye.com

Chapter 1

Rebecca nervously glanced at the two-story hotel. It would have to do. With gloved hands, she reached down and brushed the dust from her skirts, then lifted her hands to push strands of dark brown hair that had seen better days back under the brim of her hat. Squaring her shoulders, she grabbed the small carpetbag and marched across the street with a determination seen in many pioneer women.

She would get by.

Somehow.

If it took her last breath, she'd do it!

She did it before in New York City, working in the factory along side her best friend Hannah and living in poverty in a room at the Barger's Boarding House. Back then she had made a promise to herself for a better life. No knight would ever come to her rescue, that was fairy-tales and nonsense. There had been no sweet, dear mother to tuck her in at night and read to her, either. She had done all her reading from the cold, hard window seat of the brick and mortar library when she had a chance to sneak away from the orphanage she grew up in.

When Rebecca turned of age, the orphanage had turned her out on to the cold streets of the bustling city. Without a plan she may have died there. She was smarter than average and had planned well ahead of time for the day she was tossed out like a rotten apple. She had been forced to work at the factory for a year before she left the orphanage, so Rebecca had hid a partial amount of the earnings from the nuns. She had seen it before, how coming of age was a terrible way to homelessness.

Not for Rebecca. She didn't even know her last name until the nuns at the orphanage told her they adapted the name Williams for her. She accepted it as fact even though it probably was made up. Those days were long gone. She wasn't living that life any longer. It had been awhile since she felt the cold streets of New York City under her boots. For all it was worth, she would make a new life here in the state of Texas.

In New York she had been living in a shady, cheap boarding house, afraid for her life many times as she made her way home in the dark at night. One evening after fleeing from a hoodlum, she had decided she didn't want to be a slave to factory work in New York City for the rest of her life in a hot sweatshop. Rebecca had reluctantly answered an advertisement to become a mail order bride, thinking her days of living like an orphan were over.

That hadn't panned out at all. The horrible man had even fooled the mail-order matchmaking services she had hired. Mr. Abbott had lied through his rotten teeth, claiming to be a widow with two children and a farm.

The letters he had written were so sweet they stole her heart at first. She had thought they would be a perfect match and she'd finally have a home with a yard and a family of her own. Rebecca had even looked forward to the unknown adventure of traveling westward on the railroad.

Unfortunately, it wasn't meant to be. What she got was hood-winked. When she had reached her destination, four ladies stood alongside her on the platform waiting for their husbands-to-be. To the surprise of each mail order bride, their husband-to-be happened to have the same name, John Abbott. As the four women put two and two together, realizing they had been duped, a man came towards them with spaces between his stained teeth. He was nothing more than a hustler! They all tried to scatter and flee but the four women were caught easily enough and with the help of another man were forced into a wagon against their will.

Rebecca knew how to get around the streets of New York City without being caught so it was nothing to find a hiding place easily enough. The small western town she was in was filled with areas that easily let her fit into crevices without being seen. She had waited for what seemed like hours crunched into a tight space between two identical buildings until the man gave up and took the other women away in the guarded wagon.

Shaking with fear of being caught, Rebecca heard his voice loud and clear as he led the wagon away from town. "I own you!" he had yelled in to the street. He said she owed him for the train ticket and he would collect. He laughed out loud, his scruff, mean voice causing a shudder and gasp to escape her. A hand flew over her mouth. She pressed it tight against her mouth so she didn't give her position away. She wouldn't let him get to her. From her hiding place, she watched one of the girls yell out to a passer-by for help until that evil man turned from the bench and back-handed the frightened lady across the face. The poor girl's head flung to the side and she sobbed uncontrollably until he yelled for her to stop crying or he'd do it again.

No one tried to rescue those poor, helpless women. Rebecca almost gave up her hiding spot to confront the townsfolk who wouldn't lift a finger to help, but stopped herself before she revealed herself and became a victim like them. Rebecca was not about to stay in this horrible place where people could care less about another human being. She had enough money tucked away for a train ticket away from here and to get by until she found work. She would go somewhere safe.

Rebecca found out the man was nothing more than a procurer of soiled doves. He was bringing women west under the impression they were to become brides when all he wanted them for was to work in his brothel. He even sold some in traveling auctions like caged animals. She had accidentally overheard two passengers who were leaving town talk about the man who claimed to own her. They said everyone knew what he was doing. She gritted her teeth in anger. If the townsfolk knew this was happening, why hadn't they stopped him?

Fear and loathing didn't stop Rebecca from trying to embark on the first train out of the railroad town. She would not become another man's property. Not a chance!

Now, here she was, in the city of Dallas, Texas, staring at a bigger than life three-story hotel across the street from the train depot. The dust from her long train ride lingered in her hair and face. Finding a bed to sleep in was priority, even if she had to dispense some of her stashed money. There was no sleeping on the train, even though her eyes had drooped shut several times. The rattling and noise from the loud steel ride made sleeping soundly all but impossible.

She would afford herself one night in a nice hotel, wash up and then start a plan of action first thing in the morning. She had to wire Miss Aloise and let her know what that horrible man had done so the agency didn't send anyone else. She hoped and prayed he wasn't in this city. Staying low and hiding in plain sight was her best course of action for now.

Rebecca Williams was used to being alone. She would be her own knight in shining armor. A crooked smile played on her mouth as she took a step on the dusty path to the hotel.

"You want me to do what?"

The older lady smiled. Sweetly. Too sweetly if his opinion was of any value.

Her delicate gloved hands were placed into the palms of his own hardened ones as he led them across the dance floor. Instead of answering, she pushed back and twirled, giving him no choice but to follow her lead. She was no pushover. He had heard about Miss Addie even before he stepped foot in Wichita Falls. She was one of the cornerstones of the small, budding city.

She was also a busybody.

A matchmaking busybody who practically brought every couple in this small town together in one way or another.

Who was now offering her services to him.

"You heard me right, Mr. Montana. Or, should I say Sheriff Jackson Montana?"

His feet came to a halt. "I'm not the Sheriff, yet."

"All it takes is one more vote. Guess who has the deciding one?" She smiled her sweet smile once again, drilling those dark eyes into the depths of his very soul. She released her hand from the palm of his and wiggled her fingers in the air.

"Figures," he mumbled under his breath, an understanding of what she was doing hitting him full force. He had wondered why they hadn't finished the voting process. Maybe it was because the committee had something else in store for whoever became the new sheriff. It looked like she was about to offer him the position under dire circumstances. "You can't bribe me, Miss Addie. I don't care who you are. I've gotten along just fine all my life. Don't insult me by trying to buy me." Jackson was about to turn away when he felt her warm, ageing hand on his arm.

"I'm sorry." Her simple words spoke volumes. She sounded sincere enough. "I have more respect for you than that. My apologies, please."

He hesitated a moment before he turned back. He could at least listen to what she had to say. Taking her hand in his, he picked up where they left off, leading expertly across the dance hall. "My apologies as well, Miss Addie, but, I don't want to get married."

She tilted her head. "Why not, sir? You will soon be the new Sheriff in town. Your reputation as a gunfighter is impressive. Your history as a soldier will make this town feel safer. There may even be a chance to become mayor some day. I know you grew up in an orphanage. It must have been a lonely life for one so young, no?"

Jackson felt the distant dread begin to rise as memories of life in an orphanage overwhelmed him for a moment. He didn't like to talk about his past or have anyone else discuss it, not even with this dashing woman who could charm the pants off anyone, young or old. Before he could say so, she continued on in her steady voice.

"I get the feeling you don't like to talk about your childhood, but, may I just say that the only reason I know about your situation is because I am indeed on the town committee and read the application and hiring questionnaire. I don't gossip so no one will ever know you were an orphan and sent out on the mercy train when you were so young. But, that is precisely the reason I have the perfect solution."

Jackson grinned. "You are something else, Miss Addie. Go ahead, feed me your poison."

She smiled back, her ageing skin crinkling a bit around the eyes. "I assure you, when you find out who I want you to marry, you will be so happy."

"Is that a fact? Now why don't you spill it then, Ma'am." He twirled her around as the music picked up for the final chorus.

She stopped dead in the middle of the dance floor and grabbed his arm. "Follow me, this is serious." She didn't wait but scooted through the crowd of people dancing and milling around on the sidelines and stood away from the crowd, facing him. The older woman's face turned dead serious. "Here's the deal, Mr. Montana. In order to save a ladies reputation, I am looking for a man who will marry her right away and rescue this sweet woman, to boot. Whom, I may add, is a close friend of one of our important townsfolk. Although, I would keep that part quiet until she is returned here unharmed."

"Who is she?"

Miss Addie stepped closer. "She is from your past. The girl grew up in the exact same orphanage you did in New York City. I realize you were but a child then, but you may even know her. Rebecca Williams, does that name ring a bell?"

Jackson shrugged. "Not one bell, Miss Addie. Girls and boys were in separate quarters. I tend to let that part of my past where it belongs, in the past. Now if you don't mind, I have to go."

"Please, Mr. Jackson, think about it. She is in dire straits in Dallas, waiting for someone to fetch her. The man she was supposed to marry turned out to be nothing more than a horrible, greedy sheister. I am in contact with all the matchmaking services from coast to coast. Everyone's reputation is at stake. Since I am the closest, it is my duty to get her here right away and have her married immediately."

Jackson stopped. "What makes you think you can keep her safe here?"

Miss Addie inhaled. "Why, if she were married to you, then she would never be in any harm."

"I don't intend to marry."

"Think about this. Becky is scared and alone. No one wants to feel that pain."

Jackson froze. "Did you say Becky?"

"Yes."

"From New York City?"

Miss Addie nodded, her eyes intent. "The same area you grew up in and the same orphanage."

Jackson's hairs stood on end. He could feel them through the coarse dark button down shirt he wore. It couldn't be little Becky, his best and only friend, the girl he remembered so well. The Becky he hugged that last day in the library and promised he'd be back someday and help her get away from there? He shook his head. New York City had tons of people there. There was no way it could be that Becky! Impossible!

"I can see the interest resting in your eyes, sir."

"I may have known a Becky once."

"It may be the Becky you remember. At least help me get her safely away from that horrible man."

"Why are you so interested, Miss Addie? What is this Becky person to you?"

Miss Addie sighed. At first Jackson recognized the guilt shaming her face but she quickly composed herself. "I may have taken a part in finding her a husband, only to find he fooled us all. I take my position serious, sir. This man not only duped all of the agencies across the land, but a young lady who didn't deserve it."

"I don't understand." Although, he was beginning to get the full picture.

"This horrible man is posing as a widowed farmer, going through several agencies to find brides. He's been duping many agencies for some time now, pretending he needs a bride for his motherless children. He even set up a fake address so when we inquire about him, it all looks quite legitimate. All his credentials seemed to be true to form. When the bride is sent to him, he shows his true self and they either find themselves sold in auctions or working for him in an improper way, if you get my meaning, Mr. Montana."

Jackson groaned. He did get it. This low-life wouldn't stop until he was brought to justice. He had seen it many times before. "You won't stop him, Miss Addie. He'll just start up somewhere else in another town."

"You may be right. What isn't right is leaving a poor stranded girl out on her own with nowhere to go. This may or may not be my fault but I intend to make it right. Even though I wasn't directly involved, I feel as if I am responsible for her. I need you, Mr. Montana. You have the experience to bring her back here safely. Will you do it, please?"

Jackson didn't want to. "I came to Wichita Falls to start a new life, Miss Addie."

"I understand, truly I do." She leaned in closer. "I hold the winning vote. I've done some investigating of my own, Mr. Montana. I know you are trying to escape the hangman's noose over in that awful outlaw town of Mill Ridge. That whole town is crooked. It didn't matter if you were defending that sweet family or not. Taking the position as our newly sworn in sheriff will make a big difference. We will vouch for you as a whole town if they ever come looking for you. You won't be alone."

Jackson had always been alone. He'd always found his own way, fought his own battles. War, hunger, beatings from the nuns. Somehow, he'd managed to survive through it all.

Then he showed up in Wichita Falls. From the start, the people treated him like a real person. Even though he'd only been here for a short time, he had made some friends. Friends. Like the ones who would have your back in a fight. Something he'd never had. Or, inquiring about his well-being. Now that was new to him.

At one point, a suggestion for sheriff was made. Somehow he got caught up in it and filled out the application. Now this lady standing in front of him who practically helped to run this town, was offering to back him if anything ever came of the Mill Ridge fiasco. She was promising for the whole town.

He always thought he wanted to live his entire life on his own. Since he had no love from the start, he didn't have any to give.

The town of Wichita Falls and the people in it were feeling like a real family here of late. They were getting under his skin. In his blood. He rather liked the fact he had others who seemed to give a care if he lived or died.

There had only been one other person who had ever cared.

Becky.

He had never forgotten her. Even though at one point, he had returned as promised to find her betrothed to someone else. He had left then, never to step foot in New York City again. His intentions were to free her from the orphanage, offer his hand in marriage to get his best friend away from the horror of life there. When he found out she was already taken, he knew turning away was the right thing to do. She deserved so much more than a no good drifter like him. Besides, he was eleven years old when he had left that city behind the first time. He couldn't expect her to remember or even wait until he returned. There was no way she'd hold on to a promise he made so many years earlier that he would be back for her.

He was eighteen when he returned the second time. She had been sixteen when he went back only to find her engaged to someone else.

Now, he had a chance to see her again.

If it was truly her.

Intuition said it was.

His head said no. It couldn't be.

Yet, he had to know.

He sighed then raked a hand through his hair. Jackson nodded. "I'll do it."

A knowing smile played upon the older woman's face. As if she knew all along he couldn't say no. "Thank you."

Jackson closed his eyes, sending a dire prayer to the man upstairs.

Chapter 2

Rebecca pushed the covers back the moment the sun peeked through the drafty windows. The make-shift dark curtains didn't do a good job hiding the sun. She pushed them aside, letting in rays of sunshine, placing a smile upon her face. Indeed, it was a glorious morning. She was alive and grateful.

The street stirred. People milled around the shops lining the wooden board walks. She peeked out the window, taking her hand and rubbing it against the dirt spots on the window, making it worse. Looking around, Rebecca found a small towel on the night stand and began the task of cleaning the dirty window. She poured a small amount of water from the pitcher in to her wash basin, dipped the rag and began to clear a large area, enabling a large enough space to see the street below. Obviously, the windows were not a priority. Someone should clean them before letting out a room, she thought to herself. Especially in such a top-notch hotel like this.

Satisfied, Rebecca washed her hands and stood by the window, people watching. She wanted to make sure there was no sign of that horrible man, John Abbot, if that was his real name, which she doubted. Wagons burst on the scene, trampling through the dirt streets, the clopping of horses hooves loud enough for Rebecca to hear as far as the third floor. She tried to push open the window but it wouldn't budge. Frustrated, she turned to get dressed, determined to start her day with a bit of fresh air.

Luckily, her carpetbag wasn't lost back at the other stop. She sighed, blowing out air from deep in her lungs as she dressed in her dusty skirt and blouse, swiping at yesterday's filth the best she could. Not owning much never occurred to her, she always decided to be satisfied with what she had and tried to make the best of it, in hopes that someday she'd have a better life. In light of her soon-to-be husband turning out to be a no good rotten, lyin' scallywag without a conscience, the desire of having a family and taking care of children were feared to be a thing of the past.

Rebecca had enough of wanting a life with a man for now! She had learned a long time ago to depend on herself, and she had. Watching how the orphanage had turned out others had made her determined it wouldn't happen to her and she prepared for years for the day when she would be asked to leave. In a way, the excitement of living on her own without harsh punishment pushed her even more to keep any xtra money earned hidden from the sisters at the orphanage.

She checked in her reticule to make sure her money was still there. Picking up her boot, she stuffed a large amount down inside before stepping into it. Keeping a small amount safe never hurt, and would reassure her if anything happened.

Taking a long, deep breath, she turned the porcelain knob on the door and began her trek downstairs. Stopping at the front desk, a different man from the one when she checked in turned to face her.

Young and determined to please his customers, he held out his hand to Rebecca. "Good morning, Miss. How may I help you today?"

Rebecca took his hand, giving it a firm shake. The man behind the desk lifted his brows.

"Well, sir, may I speak to the manager of the hotel, please?"

His brows furrowed. "That would be my father, Mr. Douple. I'm sorry to say he isn't here at the moment. May I help you?"

Rebecca placed a finger at her chin. She tapped her booted heel a few times, pretending to be contemplating whether to speak to him regarding her problem. "Sir, I assume you have the same authority to take matters into your own hands, so, I would like to offer my assistance."

The young man clasped his hands together. "How so? We are not hiring at the moment."

"I do believe you may want to reconsider, sir." She put both gloved hands on the counter and pressed against it, lowering her voice. "There is terrible dirt and grime on my windows. I had to clean them before I was able to look out upon the street. This is a fine hotel, but someone is not doing their job."

The young man's cheeks actually reddened. "I am so sorry for the lack of cleanliness. To be honest, we did have to fire two housekeepers in the last several weeks. Our new one is in training. But, no worries, I'll have someone take care of this right away, even myself if need be."

Rebecca gave him a wide smile. "No, sir. It is cleaned. I did it myself."

His face contorted. "We can't have our guests cleaning the windows! What kind of message does that send out to our customers! I apologize profusely." He reached for the cash register. "Let me give your money back for your night's stay here."

Rebecca held up her hand before placing it over his. His blush was disturbingly adorable. "I'm not sure what to call you, sir."

He cleared his throat, his eyes wide open. "Jack. Jack Douple, ma'am."

Rebecca almost giggled at his squeaky voice. She almost felt sorry for the fellow. "I do not want my monies returned. However, I do have a proposition for you. Since you do need more help, I'd like to offer my services as a housekeeper for a discount on my room. I would love to stay here until further notice."

And that was how Rebecca got to live at one of the finer hotels in Dallas, Texas. She paid a smidgeon of the full price for helping to clean windows, run errands and occasionally serve food in the restaurant. Mostly, she stayed behind the scenes, working out of the public eye. She didn't want to be seen by Abbott if he happened to come to town. There was still a trepidation of fear surrounding her at all times. Rebecca didn't like having to constantly search a room or check the street to make sure the way was clear. It became a habit non-the-less.

Sooner or later, she knew her time here would end. She had sent Miss Aloise another message, letting her know where she ended up, hoping it was received by now and someone was on their way to fix this. Rebecca had demanded Miss Aloise come to her rescue, after all, it was their fault she was in this mess. Not that she couldn't survive on her own, she had done so living in one of the largest cities on the east coast. But, when a wrong was done it was only proper to make it right.

Rebecca still had dreams of becoming a bride with a family. When Miss Aloise sent a telegram responding to her plea, the matchmaker promised to fix her up with someone she could trust.

Rebecca no longer trusted anyone, not even the matchmaking service. But her dream of a family and a husband who would love her would never die. Not even after this. When she had been beaten by the nuns for being cheerful, Rebecca made up her mind so long ago that she would never lose faith in herself. That she would always choose to be positive and never give up. Those nuns were awful, trying to force her and everyone else to live in misery, but she would not do so. They had tried to break her and failed.

As she cleared a table in the dining room, a secretive smile emerged as she remembered her only solace was in the library. Sneaking away at ten years old to a place that held wonders and magnificent stories urged her to keep dreaming. She remembered sitting on the window seat caught up in a fairytale when a boy a few years older pushed his way through rows of books and sat in the corner beneath the window.

"Get out of my space," she had threatened, trying to sound mean.

He had looked up at her and grinned, an awful nasty black eye sticking out like a sore thumb. "It isn't your space," he had told her, refusing to move.

She had placed a foot against his shoulder and tried to push him from the spot. That's when he grabbed her ankle and twisted.

Rebecca was tougher than dirt. She wasn't about to give in.

"Say uncle," he had demanded.

"Never!" she had proclaimed. "If you don't let go of my foot, I'm calling Miss Parker." She was the librarian who would dismiss anyone who caused trouble. Many times Rebecca watched her take a swat at someone who was too loud.

"Is there something going on here?" Miss Parker happened to come around the corner, her horn-rimmed glasses pushed down to the tip of her nose. They were attached to a beaded necklace around her neck.

That quick her foot was released. "No, ma'am," he said.

Miss Parker tilted her head, staring directly at Rebecca. "Miss Williams?"

Miss Parker demanded her to answer. She gazed at the top of the boys head. She was a regular here and all she had to do was tell Miss Parker he was bothering her and he'd be thrown out. Yet, he hadn't hurt her. He just seemed to want a space to sit and read. She shrugged and shook her head. "Everything is fine, Miss Parker."

The librarian stiffened before taking a middle finger and pushing her glasses back up her nose. "Make sure you remain quiet, or the both of you will be gone from here like yesterdays news."

As she turned to go back to her place at the desk, her high heeled boot got caught in a crack in the floor. The librarian reached out to catch herself before she tottered to the ground. "Oh, pussyfoot!" she growled, causing Rebecca to giggle. She slapped a hand across her mouth so she wouldn't be heard.

That's when she noticed the boy's shoulders shaking. Was he that scared? *What a crybaby!* He began to hiccup as she realized he was trying hard to keep from laughing. Right before he yelled out, she slapped a hand over his mouth.

His spittle was on the palm of her hand, but she kept it there until he nodded for her to remove it, sure the librarian was far enough away. Slowly, she did. "Yuck! You spit on me!" she fumed, her nose wrinkling at the liquid on her hand. She desperately wiped it on the hem of her dress.

He turned. "I'm sorry I grabbed your foot. Did I hurt you?"

She shook her head. Dark curls bobbed around her head. She liked when she could let them bounce instead of having to tie them back in one big bun. "No. But if you want to sit here and read, you better be quiet."

"Deal."

They shook hands and it became a routine.

Each day she had slipped away to the library, he had been there, sitting in the same spot. She was curious where he lived so she asked him, making sure to keep her voice so low the librarian wouldn't hear. "Where do you live, Jackson?" He had told her his name a few days before.

"At the orphanage right up the street, but not for long. I'm going to find a job soon so I can be on my own."

"I live there, too. On the other side, away from the boys."

That's when they became the best of friends. Two orphans who understood the need to spend time in a quiet place with their thoughts. They would meet every day for over a year until one day he told her he was leaving on the mercy train.

Rebecca remembered how sad she felt that day he left.

"I told you I would get a job. This seems like it's the only way. In reality, I have no choice," he told her right before he gave her an awkward hug. She clung to him outside the library that day, sad she was losing her best friend.

He had looked back, grinning. "Someday I'll come back here for you," he told her right before he gave her a punch in the shoulder.

She tried to duck, pretending to laugh while she was aching inside so bad. Her best friend was leaving. "I doubt it. You've probably all but forgotten me already."

He turned, giving her that grin she learned to love as best friends do. "Never. I'll never forget my best friend."

The library had never been the same again.

"Miss Williams? Is there a problem?"

Rebecca shook herself, realizing she had been rubbing one spot on the wooden table while reminiscing about a time so long ago. "Oh, there is a spot that is hard to clean, but, I think I got it." She swiped the cloth one more time before turning away from the table and froze.

From where she stood, the front desk was clearly visible. That horrible man, John Abbott stood there, his eyes concentrating on his coat as he began wiping droplets of rain from the dark material. Rebecca slowly took a few steps back out of the view of the front desk. If he turned, he was sure to see her there. She had to get back to her room but the only way was by the way of the stairs.

Her throat constricted, fear edged its way up her spine. Tiny drops of sweat trickled around her hairline. Rebecca cursed herself for not leaving this hotel. She knew staying in one place for too long was dangerous. She had been waiting for Miss Aloise to do something. Rebecca should have known better. No one would rescue her. She had learned that a long time ago.

"I am famished!" his burly voice roared over the open room. "But first I need to wash some suds down at the saloon across the street. I'll be back in about an hour. Make sure to keep a plate nice and hot for me!"

Rebecca held her breath as he turned to go out the front door. She stepped forward but froze when he turned back to the desk manager. "There's a bag that needs to get up to my room. Make sure you get it there," he ordered, then slammed the front door behind him.

Rebecca didn't realize she was holding her breath until she felt the air leaving her lungs. The moment he was gone, she lifted her skirts and raced up the stairway in the main lobby.

"Miss Williams!"

She didn't have time to stop and explain. Flinging the worn carpetbag on the quilted bed, she stuffed her two dresses and nightdress inside, shoving her toiletries in a corner. Closing the bag, Rebecca raced back down the stairs, past the front desk and out the door. She glanced towards the saloon, which sat catty-corner to the giant hotel. Slipping down the alley beside the hotel, she wound her way from the backside of buildings, following an escape plan she had memorized in her head the very first day she had arrived.

Rebecca wasn't about to let anyone take her by surprise! She had mapped this route right to the train station in case she had to leave in a hurry. It was her way, always ready to make a run for it.

Because Rebecca knew she'd never have that knight in shining armor to fall back on. It was all up to her.

John Abbot strolled out of the saloon the moment she took a step onto the platform at the train station. She ducked behind the office building, waiting a few moments before taking a peek to see if he was still standing there. When it seemed clear, she went and stood at the counter, tapping on the glass to get the man's attention. When the ticket man slid the window open, she hurriedly asked him when the next train is due.

"In about twenty minutes. Don't tally if you plan to be on it because this stop is like quicksilver. The train stops to unload and load up and it's off again. Five minutes tops, ya hear?"

"I'll take a ticket."

"Where to, Ma'am?"

"Where ever this takes me," she told him, shoving a pile of money through the window.

He whistled as he checked the schedule. "Why, this amount can take you as far as Californy."

She turned to see John Abbott looking up and down the dusty street. "So be it," she said. "Give me the ticket. Hurry."

Sticking the paid ticket in her reticule for safe keeping, Rebecca moved to the other side of the station, where those cold eyes of

John Abbott would not see her. Fear like she had never felt scorched her from the tip of her toes to the top of her head.

She kept glancing at the tracks, willing the train to be early. Fat chance of that, she thought, grimacing to herself. Taking another peek around a large pole, Rebecca's stomach fell when she saw him heading towards the train station.

The horrible man stomped down the street as if he owned the town, his boots stirring the dust in the street, a tiny trail of dust bellowing around him.

Her ears perked up when she heard the distant sound of a whistle blowing through the air. Fear like nothing she had ever felt penetrated her whole body, she wasn't sure the train would get here on time. Abbott was getting closer, his booted heels picking up speed when his head shot to the train closing in.

Did Rebecca have any chance of getting on that train? She didn't even have money to live in californy but that didn't matter. What did was her high-tailing it out of this town so Abbott didn't try to take what he thought he deserved. He was a horrible man.

Clenching her carpetbag closer, the rumbling of the tracks caused her to sigh out loud. She took a step back when her worst fear came true. Abbott was now standing on the platform, his beady eyes peeled on her. "Stop that woman from getting on the train!" He smashed a fist to the window of the teller, demanding the man to pay attention.

The glass window slid open. The teller was pale, his voice shaking when he spoke. "She bought a ticket," he told Abbott.

"Where to?" he roared.

"Californy," the teller said, tossing her under the wagon.

Rebecca could hear the conversation, their voices were so loud in her ears even though the train's heavy metal wheels were squealing so loud. She glared at the teller, even though he didn't have a clue she was trying to stay out of the horrible man's clutches.

The frightened teller pointed straight to her, regardless of her hand motions to not tell.

Abbott placed a hand on his hip as if he were going to go for the pistol hanging on his side. Fear reared its ugly head as she gripped onto the carpetbag and took another step backwards. She was vicariously close to the edge of the platform but she'd rather fall and break her neck than be a victim of this man's horrible deceptions.

"You there! Stop! Do not get on the train!" Abbott ordered.

"Please! Go away!" she shouted above the squealing brakes as the train came to a stop. Rebecca knew without a doubt she could not get on the train. He would come after her knowing where she was going. He had said he would find her and she'd pay!

The only money she had was spent on one ticket out of desperation. It had been a horrible mistake. A costly one.

Rebecca didn't know what to do.

Her life was going from bad to worse.

Did she even value her life any more?

What did she have to look forward to?

Life with a horrible man who would sell her to the highest bidder or use her as a soiled dove? There was no way she was going to give up and yet it seemed as if she were at a cornerstone.

As her mind toiled with these thoughts, she never heard the horse and rider coming up alongside the train station. A deep voice came out of nowhere. "You're not about to give up that easily, are you?"

She shook her head. "W-what?"

As her eyes opened she saw Abbott crossing the platform, just a few feet away.

She turned to the voice just as a strong arm came out and whisked her off the platform. She flew through the air, one hand clutching her bag, the other reaching out desperately for something solid right as she landed smack dab onto a hard lap. A bold, manly voice laughed out loud as if he were enjoying her distress right before the wind blew across her face as they rode hell-bent for leather away from the train.

Chapter 3

Rebecca didn't want to remove her head nestled in the man's chest, even if he were a complete stranger. She felt his deep, steady breathing as the horse galloped away from Dallas. Trying to stay as still as possible, she sucked in the air and got a scent of leather and smoke. It was a pleasant smell, albeit a strange one. She had never been in close proximity to a man of this caliber before.

Rebecca didn't accept a hug or give one. She basically stayed to herself, keeping her distance from any close ties, a product of years of being unloved at the orphanage. It was better this way, she mused, as her body snuggled closer to her rescuer, defying the strict rules she had imposed upon herself. A longing like she'd never felt before struck her just then. It was a strange sensation, almost as if she were familiar with this stranger.

Or, should she say, her rescuer? A tiny giggle formed way deep down inside and began to build up until her shoulders began to shake. How ironic that she was rescued by a man on a horse. Almost like a knight in shining armor, except she wasn't prone to fairy tales or their ilk. She was a self-made woman, one who would get out of ire situations on her own.

Except for this one time.

She felt the rumble of his deep voice roll across her cheek. "You think this is funny?"

Immediately, her giggles stopped. "I'm sorry," she tried to shout above the noisy pounding of the horses hooves as they raced across the Texas prairie, taking them further and further away from the train station.

Should she be frightened of this man who whisked her away from a dangerous hooligan? Honestly, the only thing she felt was safe.

Rebecca tried to twist her head to look behind them to see if Abbott followed. Relieved the coast was clear, the only thing she saw was dust billowing around them, leaving a cloudy view of the open land.

"Hang on tight!" he ordered, the hard muscles of his strong arm pulling her even closer, if that were possible. Rebecca tensed as the horse picked up speed, galloping so fast she cried out in surprise, her arms automatically wrapping around the man's torso. She bunched her fists against the long, leather coat he wore and held on for dear life, her face crushed against his chest.

It wasn't long before they came to a stop in a grove of trees along the banks of a flowing river. "Home is just across the ridge up yonder," he motioned towards a grassy knob. "We'll cross the river further up after a small rest for the horse."

The man slid off the saddle as if it were the most natural thing to do. He lifted her off as if she had the weight of a goose feather, setting her firmly on the ground. A strange sensation came over Rebecca, as if she felt lost without his warmth.

"Thank you for saving me from that horrible man," she whispered, grateful and yet cautious. Rebecca followed behind as the horse and rider made their way to the riverbank, staying close in case Abbott decided to appear out of nowhere, a fear that had crossed her mind.

The stranger seemed aware of her concerns. "Don't worry, by the time he hitches a horse to come after us, our trail will be cold." The man let the reins go as the horse slurped fresh flowing water at the river's edge.

Watching the two, she made a decision not to worry. Fear had no place in her life. Rebecca looked around, the spotted green and brown prairie stretching for miles, the steady stream of crystal water flowing down river. Her mind was immersed in the serenity of nature until his voice rang out.

"Aramis, be gentle," he warned.

Rebecca looked up to see the horse's head lift up as a yellow and black butterfly landed on the tip of its ear. He twitched and slowly shook his head as the beautiful creature flew off. She took a few steps closer to the enormous beast and placed a hand gently on his neck, no longer afraid. If this gentle giant could be so cautious with a butterfly, there was no need to be nervous. "Aramis," she repeated the name. "One of the three most formidable musketeers of the age."

The man stood beside her and nodded. She felt his eyes on her as she ran her hand along the horse's mane.

She smiled, concentrating on the beautiful mane. "I remember a long time ago, there was a boy who loved this book about the musketeers. I remember how his face would light up as he read each page."

Rebecca felt the man suck in a deep breath, yet she continued to pet the horse, immersed in her memories. "He invaded my space at the library back then, but we grew to be best friends."

"I recall the book, and can quote it page by page. It was about the poor nobleman who risks all to travel to Paris to join the Musketeers and defend the regiment."

Rebecca laughed aloud, the memory so sharp." It was so exciting to hear the story, day after day. It was a book filled with adventure and intrigue, along with romance."

"I clearly remember the adventure and intrigue part of the story."

"He was my best friend back then."

"Who? The young hero of the book, d'Artagnan?"

She laughed, her eyes closed now as the old, childhood memories came back full force. "No. His name was Jackson," she told him. "He had the bluest eyes that I will never, ever forget. They were the boldest blue, hidden by the longest dark lashes a boy could have. I think kids made fun of him, called him pretty eyes, that's why he was always alone. Jackson was my friend, we would read our books together, under the window seat of the big library, every single day. I missed him terribly after he was gone. He left on a mercy train one afternoon."

She opened her eyes to realize she wasn't back at the library of her youth, but in a field of greenery, telling a total stranger her deepest life's memories. She shook herself, determined to remove the flow of sadness that now surrounded her. "I wonder what ever happened to him?"

When there was silence, she turned her head to the man beside her who had removed the hat that recently hid most of the features on his face.

The boldest, bluest eyes watched her with trepidation. Long, black lashes surrounded the blue orbs.

Rebecca stared. Hard. Her eyes roamed every inch of him from the top of his dark head to the tips of his dirty leather boots. Was that a badge on his gun belt? "Who are you?"

He flicked a finger over the badge. "Name's Sheriff Jackson Montana, ma'am."

"It's you then? Jackson?" Her hand went to her throat. So many years had passed, how could she be sure it was truly him? Rebecca swayed back and forth a moment before she found her footing. She remembered thinking how odd it was she made fun of the other ladies when they swooned over something and here she was doing the same. Locking her knees, determination forced its way to the front, assuring she would not act like a weak woman. After all, she was strong and independent.

Jackson smiled.

The moment he did all doubt was removed. She had never forgotten the way one side of his face produced a small dimple in his cheek. It hadn't changed even after he had grown up. It was her Jackson, her best friend. He had been found at last.

She let out a whoop and flung her arms in the air, clapping them together. "I didn't ever think I would see you again after you left on the train. Let me look at you."

Jackson placed his hat back on his head and grinned. "I suppose you'll be seeing a whole lot more of me in the near future."

He took a step back.

She tilted her head still smiling with excitement. "I hope so."

"Considering we've more or less been thrown together, I am assuring you that is an accurate statement."

"Thrown together? How so?"

"I was ordered here by Miss Adeline of Wichita Falls, where you will find right around the bend over yonder. You were promised a husband after the last mail order fiasco and I was selected to be that husband."

"Wait! What! My best friend as my husband! That's unheard of!" Although, saying so made a smile so wide spread across her face she was about to explode! Rebecca pressed her hands together in front of her. She wanted to jump up and down and throw her arms around Jackson but held herself back. Ladies didn't act like trollops, even if she wanted to give him a big old hug.

"Looks like it's so, Becky. Seems I got hood-winked into taking you as my mail order bride."

The words instantly stopped her from throwing her arms around him. Both hands went to her hips instead. "Hood-winked! Why, Jackson Montana, if you think being married to me will be so awful, then why did you agree!"

He came closer to her as she took a step back, his blue eyes staring into her own. A wisp of his warm breath fell across her cheek. "I had no plans to get married until Miss Adeline more or less made a proposal that was hard to refuse."

She was standing too close in proximity to this man who had been her dear friend at a time in their lives when all they had was each other. Today, he was like nothing she ever imagined. Tall, dark and handsome, and a sheriff to boot. Marriage to him would not be so bad, assuming he would allow her to keep her independence. "I, I don't understand."

His knuckles brushed across her cheek. Rebecca's eyes widened at Jackson's bold move. "When Miss Addie, that's what we call her, proposed her offer, I simply refused. But then, she told me my intended bride's name was Becky from the same orphanage in New York and I had to know."

His hand cupped her chin as he stared into her eyes.

She couldn't look away. "I can't marry a sheriff," she whispered, entranced by those dark lashes and deep blue orbs.

"It's destiny, Becky. We belong together."

Shaking herself, Rebecca smiled. "I doubt that, Jackson. We were children back then, thrown together against all odds. Besides, I have decided to become an independent woman."

Jackson grinned. "Fine with me, Becky. You have my permission once we are married to do so."

She giggled. "I have a feeling you had no intention of a marriage. Why did you say you were hoodwinked?"

"Miss Addie is part of the town committee. She had the last vote to cast to decide if I were to become sheriff. Against my will, I allowed her to bribe me into coming for you."

"Because you wanted to be sheriff you agreed to come rescue me from that awful man?" That didn't sit too well with Rebecca. She wasn't going to marry a man for that reason.

Jackson took her by the hand as they walked along the riverbank. His long coat brushed against her skirt. "I wanted to be sheriff, yes, that part is true. But, more than that, I wanted to know if the Becky she mentioned was you."

Rebecca stopped and turned to him. "What if it wasn't me? What then, Jackson Montana?"

He grinned. "I'd be married to the wrong Becky. A promise is a promise."

She stared at him, not knowing what to think. On one hand, he blindly came to her rescue, hoping against all odds it was the girl he remembered from the library. On the other hand, if it wasn't her, he would honor his word and still marry. After what she had been through with John Abbott, it was refreshing to find a man with honor. A big smile began to spread across her face. "It happens to be your lucky day, then."

Jackson grabbed the tip of his hat and threw it in the air. He let out a whoop so loud, she playfully placed her hand across his mouth to quiet him down. He picked her up and swung her around, as she laughed and laughed.

At least one of her dreams were to come true. "How soon do we get married?" she asked, wanting to shed the horror of the past few weeks and move on to a better life.

Jackson helped her back on the horse. He pulled out a stopwatch and flipped it open. "I'd say in about four hours. No sense putting it off now that we found each other."

The reality of making her dreams come true was finally sinking in. Not only was she getting married after all this time, but, it was to her childhood best friend. Rebecca felt like the luckiest girl alive as they rode in to the town of Wichita Falls.

<> <>

Jackson swore under his breath. He was the new sheriff and yet this little missy was bossing him around as if she were his ma! They weren't even married yet. From the moment they reached town and he heard her cries of delight at the variety of buildings and shops laid out before her, she began to throw out orders like a general in an army.

"Jackson, if we are to be married, you need a bath and a suit. Jackson, you will have to find me a place to clean up. Jackson, how am I going to marry in this old outfit?"

Right there in the middle of the street, in front of God and everyone, he gave her a shaking down. No wife of his was going to sound like an old harpy. "Now you listen here, Becky, you can't go ordering me around like this. Do you know how it sounds?"

"Why, Jackson, I'm only asking so we can have a nice wedding on such short notice. Why, don't you want us to have a nice wedding?"

Jackson grabbed her waist and pulled her close right there in the middle of the street. With both hands, he placed one on each side of her face and lowered his mouth to hers, intending to shut her up with a kiss.

Except the moment their lips touched, a yearning so deep went through him, it shocked him, too. Her arms snaked around his neck, pulling him closer. He had to force himself to break the kiss, otherwise they would miss their own wedding.

She gazed at him in complete shock and disbelief. With wide eyes, the back of her hand slowly slid across her mouth. There were no words. No orders. A look of complete and utter surprise travelled over her face. Jackson slid from the horse, his boots planted firmly on the ground as he helped her off.

He took her shaking hand as they walked towards Miss Addie's boarding house. She muttered something audible when Miss Addie introduced herself and told her to sit down for a cup of tea. Jackson left her there, sitting at Miss Addie's table, her face pale and drawn. She barely acknowledged him when he told her he'd see her in a few hours at the church.

Jackson stood on the wooden porch, a bit stunned himself. He tipped his hat to a driver guiding a wagon through the dust covered street. In a few hours, he'd be married to Becky and his whole life would be changed. As he stepped off the porch, he grinned. At least he knew how to quiet the woman.

A kiss.

He would kiss her all day long if that was the reaction she got from one kiss.

He tipped his hat at another family as he walked towards the sheriff's office. At one time he dreaded the day he would have to marry. Now, he was looking forward to it.

He had to give Miss Addie credit. She had found Becky for him, after all these years. She had been the only stability in his life back then. Would she be able to bring that back or would his life now be all chaos as a married man?

Jackson didn't know what the future would bring. He did know one thing, he was going to enjoy every bit of it.

At least, before he was found out. The odds to anyone from that lying, corrupt town finding him here was like finding a needle in a haystack. As long as he stayed away from Mill's Ridge, he was safe. He vowed to keep Becky safe as his new bride. He'd have to tell her about it, but not yet. He wasn't ready to relive that part of his past.

All he wanted right now was to marry his best friend and spend his night putting that look of wonder on her face again and again.

Chapter 4

"I do."

"You may now kiss your bride. Although," the Reverend hesitated, "in recent ceremonies we've had here, some of the couples got carried away. We ask that you save the maddening kisses for later." The minister's wife stood behind him to the side, holding a small bouquet of flowers against her breast. Rebecca watched as the woman lifted them in front of her face as she tried to hide a smile that played across the older woman's cheeks.

They exchanged a friendly glance before she felt her new husband's mouth touch hers, barely. It was a quick kiss, unlike the one that made her swoon earlier. Yes, swoon. Like never in her life swoon. Rebecca had no idea how she would recover from it but Miss Addie had a long talk about such things earlier. It wasn't as if she heard a word Miss Addie had said, but had nodded in agreement as she had tried to distance herself from these new feelings towards her best friend.

Now, her husband.

Who was staring at her with an all knowing smile on his face.

She swallowed, then dug in her sleeve to retrieve a silky handkerchief to dab across her brow.

"Congratulations, Mr. and Mrs. Montana!" Reverend Daniel Conner announced. "Miss Addie, who is your witness as well as your hostess, has secured the hotel's ballroom for an afternoon wedding reception. Let's go eat!"

Jackson took his wife's arm and ploughed through the small gathering to be the first one through the door. Others began to follow him to Lily and Ben Dawson's hotel down the street.

Rebecca turned to her new husband. "Mr. Montana?"

He gave her another one of those charming grins. "Mrs. Montana, let's see what all the fuss is about."

They walked past the mercantile and the saloon. Jackson promptly steered her away from a cowboy making his way to the entrance of the drinking establishment. He tipped his hat and tightened his hold, his way of letting the cowboy know the lady was his.

Rebecca hadn't missed the exchange. It made her feel warm inside, knowing Jackson wanted everyone to know he was her protector. Another giggle erupted before she could stop herself.

"Now what is that about?" he asked gently, helping her over a small puddle so her boots wouldn't hit the water.

"I'm sorry, a bit nervous. I guess I giggle when I'm nervous."

"Nothing to be nervous about, Mrs. Jackson Montana. No need to worry about anything, ever again."

She smiled up at him, knowing he was being kind. "But you see, Jackson, its not the elements or cowboys I find myself worried about."

"Well, what is it then?"

"You."

He stopped abruptly, swinging her towards him. His hands rested gently on her shoulders. Looking into her eyes, he began to speak in a serious tone. "I will never let you come to harm, Becky. You are my best friend, more now than even when we were young. What we had will carry us through our married life. Don't you see, this marriage is indeed a blessing from above. I feel in my heart it is meant to be. No one from this town or any other will come between us."

She bit at her bottom lip nervously, causing Jackson to smile. He lifted a hand to her mouth, tracing her trembling lips with his index finger.

She sighed. "I, I know that part. It's, well, it's hard for me to explain."

"Be honest, it's all I ask."

"Tonight, well, I am nervous about tonight, our marriage bed." There. She had whispered the words that were on her mind ever since she left Miss Addie's boarding house earlier.

He wrapped his arms around her, hugging her close. "Trust me. There is nothing to worry about."

Becky nodded, then grinned. A tad embarrassed because he now knew her true emotions, she pushed her shoulders back determined to get through the afternoon without feeling shamed. "I will and I do."

He leaned over to whisper in her ear. "If you are going to be an independent woman, these things are nothing to be ashamed of. You'll see, I promise."

He led her inside, taking his time as he remarked on the décor in the lobby of the Dawson Hotel, how local artists shared their statues and paintings here. As Becky was led from the lobby to the ballroom, she was relieved to know her husband truly did have her best interests at heart. She couldn't help the giddiness inside, determined to put fear aside and enjoy the rest of the day.

John Abbot and the horrible events that had taken when she had gotten off the train weeks before were now in the past. She pushed those thoughts aside even though he had threatened to find her and make her pay. She was a married woman now. He wasn't allowed to bother her any longer.

Except those who opposed the law didn't much care about rules. A tiny thread of fear tried to push its way up until she decided to stomp it to the ground. She gazed at her new husband, noticing the strong jaw, his determined and bold features causing all the fear to flee. It was her wedding day. She was going to rejoice and be glad.

"Welcome to Wichita Falls, Mrs. Montana." A dark haired woman wearing a silky red dress and pale skin hurried to her side. A tall, handsome man stood beside her. The lady took her hands and held on to them. "It's a pleasure to see Mr. Montana married at last. I'm Lily Dawson, and this is my husband, Ben."

The man nodded, then whisked Lily away when the quartet along the far wall began to play a slow melody, her laughter renting the air. Lily's laughter faded as the two began to waltz across the floor, eyes only for each other.

Her husband held out his hand. "Care to dance, Mrs. Montana?" His eyes held her own, and his smile drew her to him like a bee to honey.

She felt silly and carefree. Without a word, she placed her hand in his and let him lead her around the floor, closer to the other couples there. With a nod, Rebecca acknowledge the other couples who smiled at them with one of her own.

It was heaven in his strong arms. This had to be a dream. She closed her eyes, letting her mind drift to a place for the lucky few. How did she become one of them?

"A penny for your thoughts?" Jackson's low voice caressed her cheek. A deep sigh escaped from down inside.

"Never in a hundred years had I thought I would be such a lucky woman. I feel as if I'm in a dream and sooner or later I'll wake up. This doesn't happen to girls like me."

He pulled her closer, his cheek against hers. "Yes it does. We are both lucky, darling. To have had such a friendship so long ago and now to rekindle it years later is a dream come true. I must admit I had my doubts I would ever find you again."

She stopped moving while the music continued on. "You looked for me? How so? I was always at the orphanage until I was thrown out the day I turned of age."

He grinned. "It's okay, Becky. I know you were betrothed to someone."

"What? You're mistaken. I've never been engaged to anyone."

Jackson's face turned grim. His eyes darkened. "Never?" he asked, clearly confused.

She shook her head. "Never. Why in the world would you think I was engaged? Except for the mail order bride fiasco, I've been alone."

Jackson mumbled under his breath. She was certain the words were too delicate for her ears was the reason he didn't dare say them out loud.

"I was duped."

"What?"

He nodded, his angry eyes glaring at the top of her head. He didn't look at her as he spoke, as if he were living a memory all over again. "When I was eighteen, I had earned enough money to leave the farm in Kansas, where I had ended up. The first thing I did was to take the train to New York to see you. I had told you I would be back for you and was determined to keep my word. Besides, I missed you. It had been six years since we had last spoken. When I got to the orphanage, I planned to whisk you away to become my bride. I stood on those cold, brick steps and knocked on the door of the girls side. Sister Mary Helen slid the door open and refused me entrance. She said you were betrothed to another man."

"No! That was a lie!" Her arms slid to his waist.

Jackson nodded. "I didn't believe her at first until she threatened to have me removed from the premises. What I just now realized is that if I had taken you from them at sixteen, they would lose two years of wages while you worked in the factory."

His stiff body was the only thing showing his hard emotions. Rebecca tried to reassure him. "I'm here now. Let's move on and forget the rest. Agree?"

He nodded, taking in a deep breath. "You are right, Mrs. Jackson. We're young, we have our whole lives ahead of us. Forget the past, just like I've always tried to do."

She smiled up at him as the music came to a stop. "Except for me. I'm a part of your past you will never be able to forget."

Jackson grabbed her and held her close in a big hug. "Becky, have I ever told you how much I missed your sass?"

"No sir, but you better start getting used to it because I'm here for good."

"Amen."

Rebecca smiled at his last remark, raising her head to the sky, thanking God for a good husband. When she gazed over the large ballroom, a figure in a dark blue coat and floppy hat that covered facial features walked briskly across the room towards the door. The mystery person turned for one last look before leaving, avoiding eye contact. She thought it was strange at first and was going to mention this to her new husband, then thought better of it. Some people were just hands down strange.

All she wanted was to have a beautiful evening as Mrs. Jackson Montana.

<> <>

Jackson noticed how Becky scrunched her brows together. He gazed across the ballroom wanting to know what caused her to look confused. As he watched a figure slide through the door, he almost went after it, wondering why someone would want to sneak through a wedding reception. "Did you see who that was?"

She shrugged. "No. Perhaps a guest from the hotel walked in here and realized there was a reception going on. My bet is they quickly tried to leave before anyone noticed they were interrupting."

Jackson pondered. Becky's answer seemed like that may be what just happened. Although he was almost always on guard because of his experience at Mill's Ridge, he had to learn to relax somewhat. It would do no one any good to become suspicious of everyone around them on his wedding day.

He swung Becky to and fro, wrapping his arms around her shoulders and placing a quick kiss upon her cheek. "Thank you."

She looked taken back. "Why?"

"For not marrying John Abbott. For running away to Dallas and for letting me rescue you."

Rebecca lifted her chin and stamped her foot. "Mr. Montana, I'll have you know I almost rescued myself. Why, I had a ticket to California in my possession. All I had to do was get on the train and I would have been safe."

Jackson rolled his eyes, but not while she could see him. There was no way she could get on the train, not with Abbott standing on the platform waiting on her.

His arms tightened around her. He wasn't sure if he loved her, but it was mighty close. Since he didn't know what love really was, he guessed he liked her an awful lot. He knew one thing. Deep down inside, he would cherish this woman and never let her come to any harm. He would give up his life to make sure she was safe. If that was love, then he guessed he was in love with his wife. He probably always was, even as a young boy.

"Can we go?" she whispered in his ear. "I'm getting tired."

Her words brought him back to the celebration in the ballroom. "Yes, let's make our leave with Miss Addie."

Jackson held her close as they made their way towards the small group in the back of the ballroom. Ben, Lily and Miss Addie were talking quietly amongst themselves when a beautiful woman glided through the crowd.

"Mr. and Mrs. Montana, may I have an interview please? It will take two minutes of your precious time?"

Jackson grimaced. The newspaperwoman was used to having her say. She had married Daniel Johnson, owner of the only newspaper in town. Jackson heard about them when he first came to town. Now he watched with amusement while she worked her way to the two of them.

"Charity Ashwood, at your service." She held out her hand, shaking each of theirs in a brisk manner. "I'll cut to the chase since I know the two of you are anxious to go home. Rumors are the two of you met many years ago while being incarcerated at an orphanage in the big city. Is this true?"

Jackson shook his head. "Miss Charity, of course it is true. How did you get this information so quickly."

Her eyes widened as if insulted. Her chin lowered. "Sheriff, I'll have you know it is my job to find these things out. I am verifying the information because I am the top newspaperwoman in Wichita Falls and beyond."

Rebecca smiled. "Miss Charity. It's been a long day. We've been chased by a bad man, escaping from his clutches by the skin of our teeth and I am ready to go home. If you want a story, how about tomorrow at noon? I will answer any and all questions then. Come for tea."

"Perfect. I was about to question you more. I'll see you then." She shook hands again and marched out of the ballroom, stopping to give Lily a hug.

Jackson smiled at his bride. "I don't think anyone has ever stopped an interview with Miss Charity so quickly."

"She seems like a lovely woman. I want to get to know her but it has been a long day."

The undercurrent in her voice pushed Jackson to take their leave. As they stepped on to the street, he wrapped an arm around her shoulders. "My office is across from the saloon, so I may have to check on the deputy sometime later on. But for now, my cabin is right down the street and around the corner."

The two strolled arm in arm past Miss Addie's towards the end of the street, where they made a right turn and crossed the street to the small cabin there. It was a one story structure, quite small with a large porch out front.

Jackson felt her shiver. "Are you cold?"

"No, I'm simply fearful of what's to come."

At least she was honest. "No need to be. Do you trust me?"

She nodded. "I do."

He picked her up, taking the steps one at a time as a nervous giggle erupted from her soft lips. He stopped at the door. "Welcome home, Mrs. Montana."

Then he swept open the door, and took her across the threshold before she could have any more second thoughts.

Chapter 5

"Sheriff Montana! Sheriff Montana!" A harried voice called from the street.

Jackson didn't want to wake up. He sucked in a deep breath and slid from the feather bed, careful not to wake his sleeping wife. As he got dressed, his hand slid open the curtain to see who was raising cain outside his home. Dressed more like a cowboy than an officer of the law in faded brown pants, a long shirt, short vest and a droopy cowboy hat, the deputy held a sheet of paper above his head, slashing it through the air as if it were from the President himself.

He wrapped his knuckles on the window to let Johnson Tanner know he heard.

"Is everything alright?" His wife's sweet voice echoed through the bedroom like a dove singing its morning song.

"Go back to sleep, darling. My deputy is calling me. I'll be back in a while."

"I'll have no difficulty with that."

Her eyes fluttered shut by the time he made it back to the bed. Little puffs of air escaped from her mouth, an almost serene like look on her beautiful face. Leaning over, Jackson brushed his mouth over her brow, grinning, remembering their wedding night. After all the talk of being scared of what was to come, she sure wasn't shy once she found out what truly happens in a wedding bed.

He wanted to stay behind and spend the day with his wife but knew there was a days work ahead. Closing the door on their little cabin, Jackson strolled to the anxious deputy. "What in tarnation is so important you have to wake me up?"

"I'm sorry, but Miss Addie sent this to me before the sun rose over the horizon. She said perhaps you should know right away." He shoved the paper at Jackson, the dread in his voice crackling like an open fire in the middle of the prairie.

Jackson snatched it from his hand, reading the headline blaring at him from the front page of the local paper.

The deputy piped up. "Can they ride in here and do something like this?"

The Sheriff shook his head. "Not in my town they won't!"

"We gonna run 'em out of town, Sheriff Jackson?"

Jackson grunted. "If we have to, yes. First things first. Let's keep an even head on our shoulders and find out how this happened."

The deputy followed on Jackson's heels as they made their way across town to the newspaper office. He hoped Daniel Ashwood was there. He didn't rightly want to discuss the impending matter with Daniel's wife, who was the newspaperman's partner in the only printing business in town.

Just as he was thinking how awkward it would be, Mrs. Ashwood came out of the office like a speeding locomotive. She nodded to the men and clammored her way down the few steps, throwing an apology at them so fast and quick they barely had time to acknowledge her. "Sorry, gentlemen, you'll have to see my husband. A big story awaits!"

Jackson, relieved for the most part, stomped up the steps, pushing his way inside. "Daniel!" he growled, angry at the newspaper man for even allowing such jargon in his paper.

Daniel sat at a big desk by the large picture window, his head down, glasses teetering on the tip of his nose. He looked up and smiled when he saw Jackson.

Except the sheriff was in no mood to be cordial. Taking long strides to the big desk, he slammed the newspaper down on top of papers that scattered in all directions at the interruption. "What's this all about?"

Daniel pushed his reading glasses up before turning the paper his way. "I am supposing you are speaking of the auction?"

"You know darn well that's what has me sore, Daniel!"

The newspaperman stood. "I'm afraid it's the right of the entrepreneur to place an ad in my paper. What kind of newspaper owner would I be if I were to make judgement on what is placed here?"

Jackson leaned closer to Daniel. "I am the sheriff in this town. How am I supposed to answer to this?"

"Well, I didn't say as a town we have to accept this type of shenanigans. I just report on what is happening."

Deputy Tanner tried to put in his two cents. Jackson almost forgot about him. "You tell 'em, Sheriff. Run them out of town when they get here! We don't want no riff-raff like that in Wichita Falls!"

The clutter of horse's hooves stopped in front of the newspaper office. Jackson glanced through the dusty window to see Miss Addie grab a parasol and make her way up the steps. Dread seeped in stronger than the aroma at the stables on an overly humid day.

Her voice permeated across the room. "Mr. Ashwood, a word please!"

"Get in line then, Miss Addie. Sheriff is questioning my reporting skills as well."

"This nonsense needs taken out of the paper immediately. We can't have this going on in our town. We've fought so hard to have a clean, respectable place for families to live."

Daniel Ashwood stood his ground as she gave him what for. "I'm sorry, Miss Addie. I'm not rescinding my story. This is what is happening and the town has a right to know and participate if they choose. You can't stop progress."

"Progress! It's inhumane! Despicable! We can't allow this in our town!"

"I agree." Jackson was not about to let this go on for much longer. He had the power to throw the auctioneer out of town and he would, lock, stock and barrel.

Addie turned to leave. "I expect all of you at the town meeting this afternoon at three. Please pass it on to everyone you know. We won't proceed with the meeting until everyone is in attendance. This may last all night so you best get moving!"

Jackson and Daniel looked at each other then grinned. "She's a feisty woman, isn't she?"

Jackson nodded. "She has a good enough reason. We can't allow this, sorry, Daniel."

"I tend to agree, Sheriff, but there's nothing I can do when someone pays me to put an advertisement in the paper. I was just bringing it to the everyone's attention, is all."

"You sure did. See you at the meeting."

Jackson left the building to watch Miss Addie storm up the steps and in to the hotel. She supposed the woman was giving fair warning to Ben and Lily to prepare the ballroom for the meeting. It was the only place big enough to hold the population of a growing town.

<> <>

"Here, here! The meeting is about to begin."

The ballroom was crowded with every single person who lived in Wichita Falls and five miles each way. It was a quarter past the hour, beings Miss Addie refused to start the meeting until every single person who lived in the town was accounted for. Per her request, Jackson had walked the board walk up and down the main street, making sure every business owner closed shop to attend. Satisfied, he returned to the hotel to wait for the meeting to start. Pungent smells of horses, sweat and sweet lilac perfume permeated the air even with the high ceilings of Ben's hotel.

"Order! Order!" Miss Addie cried out, her voice heard over top the crowd. The town committee was comprised of five men and Miss Addie. She seemed to be the one who always took the lead as the others nodded for her to start. Jackson watched from his place at the back of the ballroom, there to distil order if things got out of hand. He nodded to his deputy as the man made his way to the other side of the room, standing near a overambitious crowd who had been at the saloon earlier. They didn't need any disruptions.

Jackson whistled. "Let's all pay attention now." At his command, the room got quiet. He nodded. "Go on now, Miss Addie, let's get this show on the road."

"Thank you kindly, Sheriff Montana." Miss Addie turned to the crowd, her arm going wide as she scanned the crowd. "We have a problem. How many of you have read the morning paper?"

Some folks nodded while others raised their hands in the air. A rumble of yeahs and no's dissipated when she clapped her hands together. "Well, for those of you who can't read, perhaps a lesson in reading at our library here in the hotel would do you some good. We have classes each week. Now, back to the reason you have been called here. An auctioneer is coming to town to auction off distressed women! We can't allow selling human beings in our town like a piece of cattle."

Gasps rang through the air. Some ladies held their hands over their children's ears even though it was too late to keep them from hearing the dreaded words. Jackson glanced at his wife, watching her sweet smile turn to a horrified frown. The soft corners of her eyes crinkled as she searched for him. The moment their eyes met, Jackson knew she was worried about that son-of-a-gun Abbott who tried to steal her to do the same to her as these women he now was going to hold on the auction block. If it was indeed Abbott on the auctioneer end or another no-gooder trying to make a buck off of women's woe, they were going to stop it.

One of the men from the randy crowd stood. "I don't rightly see nothin' wrong with an auction with fine, willing women! They is hard to come by in this town!"

"Here! Here!" A few of the men raised their hands, hollering over top the crowd.

Some of the townsfolk began to raise their voices, arguing with the men who wanted to buy women from this out of town auction.

Jackson was ready for an outbreak. His body tensed as a few of the men stood to defend themselves. His fingers slowly etched to the trigger on his gun. He didn't expect to harm anyone, but if he had to whip out his pistol to quiet the room, he would do so. When the room quieted down on its own, he searched for his wife to see her standing at the front of the room, alongside Miss Addie. Her hands were pressed together, knuckles white. He wanted to storm to the front and whisk her from the meeting, protecting what she was about to reveal.

He was never more proud of his wife in that very moment.

"If I may have your attention please." Becky stood very still, waiting for the crowd to quiet even more and the men to sit down. She addressed the crowd of rowdy men first. "The women you are implying about are far from willing. I should know, I was one of them."

A few gasps rent the air. Jackson watched as she looked each man in the eye. "I didn't think I would ever have to reveal my past, but I can clearly see I must if it will save one woman from a life she never intended to live. Before I married Sheriff Montana, I was on a train to a small town in Texas to become a mail order bride."

She looked at him now for encouragement. He nodded for her to go on. "I got duped. Even though I went through a recommended agency, the intended groom fooled us all. When I arrived at my destination there was no husband to be, but a cruel man wanting to enslave me and other women to a life of horrors. I got away, but others did not. I am afraid some of those women will be here tomorrow on that wagon to be auctioned off."

Miss Addie spoke up. "I will vouch for Mrs. Montana. I knew about her predicament and asked Sheriff Montana to help her."

Jackson chewed on his bottom lip. Miss Addie knew when to jump in. He could tell the townsfolk didn't know if they should believe his wife's testimony, but the moment their trusted Miss Addie backed her up, everyone in the room changed their stance. The air seemed different at once.

"Thank you, Miss Addie. Let me make myself clear, ladies and gentleman. I understand that you do not know me well enough to believe my tale, but it's all true. This man, if it is the same one who tried to hoodwink me, has stolen these ladies and will try to sell them to the public without any qualms at all. The ladies are not willing, you are made to think they are. They may be so broken down by now or too fearful to speak. We have to save them."

The crowd roared. Even the rowdy bunch who were most likely three sheets to the wind stood up and clapped, eager to help save these women enslaved.

Jackson stepped forward. "Yesterday there was a stranger at the hotel, hiding his face. I have a feeling he snuck in to see if this was a lucrative place for an auction. Looks like it was to them. We need to stop this now! If we are all in agreement to set a trap, this town will need some help. Who is willing to help?"

One of the townsfolk stood up and hollered above the crowd. "I am. Let's show these no-gooders this town won't tolerate such goings on!"

Jackson had eyes only for his wife. He gave her a reassuring smile. She was so nervous standing up there in front of everyone. While one after another agreed to help, showing their unity, her face transformed to wonder and amazement watching these folks jump in so quickly.

She needed this town. She needed him. The truth was, Jackson was in love with her. Rebecca was his life, his wife now and he would protect her from all evil. Along with the promise of keeping this town safe, he would do even more for her. They both lived as orphans but found each other at a young age. Now, after all these years, the bond that secured them at a New York City library was still as strong as ever.

He ignored the men who stood in a cluster surrounding him and walked towards his wife, who finally smiled at him, eyes bright with unshed tears.

Chapter 6

Rebecca knew the tears were about to burst forth and dampen her cheeks as surely as she woke up this morning. The way her husband looked at her with pride and love make her realize she was home.

Wichita Falls was her home.

Sheriff Jackson Montana was home.

The love that eluded from her best friend made the tears fall all at once.

He took her outstretched hand. "Becky." With his other hand, his fingers wiped the tears. He crushed her to him, not caring if anyone paid them any mind. "I love you, Becky," he whispered in her ear.

She froze. Shivered. Knew that deep down in her heart she loved this man, the one who claimed her as a best friend when she was ten years old. She clasped his cheeks and pulled him closer so she could look in to those dark eyes. "I love you, also. More than I ever thought I could love anyone. You are my life now. You saved me from a horrible fate. I would die without you."

Miss Addie stood beside them. "Sheriff, there's much work to do if we plan to oust these hooligans from our midst."

"It can wait a few more hours, Miss Addie. My wife is hungry and I need to get her some dinner."

It was as if the man could read minds. How did he know she hadn't eaten all day, but worried herself sick the moment he told her about the auction. Rebecca peeked around his shoulder to see the older woman's reaction. She expected a stern look but found instead a grin from the woman who practically ran Wichita Falls. She turned away from them to address the crowd of men waiting for direction. "Everyone, Sheriff Montana is right. We need to take a few hours and clear our minds. Go home, have dinner and let's meet here at seven o'clock. Will that time suit, Sheriff?"

"Sounds fine to me." Jackson held out his arm. Rebecca sighed before folding her hand around his arm. "Mrs. Montana, let's go see what Jenna's Eatery has on the menu for this evening."

Rebecca couldn't help herself. When she saw Hannah, she let out a screech that turned every head in the room. Her old friend turned and stared, then began to shuffle around the crowd in the hotel's ballroom until they were hugging each other for dear life.

"Oh, Becky! I'm so happy to see you? We tried to get here earlier but my husband was held up with a problem at the ranch. What in the world are you doing here?" She looked in confusion at Jackson as he walked to his wife's side.

Rebecca laughed out loud. "This is my husband, Hannah. You may have already met him, Sheriff Jackson Montana!"

"I have and I had no clue you were here. I thought you were marrying a farmer?"

"We have so much to talk about. That didn't turn out so well, but look at you."

Hannah introduced her husband before the two couples sat together in the ballroom waiting for the committee to decide how to move forward to stop the offenders. After some talk by Miss Addie, Sheriff Montana stood up to offer suggestions on saving the women on the auction block and throwing the offenders out of town. "We will never welcome riff-raff of this sort here in Wichita Falls," Jackson said, his face stern, his eyes dark. "I am going to need everyone of you to help us pull this off and get these so called auctioneers out of our town."

"Why can't we just shoot the sonsofguns!"

Jackson groaned.

"Yeah, we can guard the road to town and shoot 'em before they get here!"

"No!"

Jackson shut everyone down with one word. When the room was once again quiet, he raised his voice. "There are women who will be in harms way if we shoot first. Our job is to make sure they are kept safe. Do I make myself clear?"

He stared down the others in the room. In that moment, Rebecca was so proud of the man she married. He would face his enemy and strike them down head on, she thought. Truly, her knight in shining armor after all. He was so brave.

"You look like you are smitten, my dear." Hannah's words were true.

She gazed over at her friend, who was grinning, admitting the truth. "I am. Do you remember how I told you about my life in the orphanage and the library?"

Hannah's eyes widened. "No! Say it isn't so?"

"It is. He is one and the same. My best friend, Jackson."

"How wonderful. I'm so happy for you, Becky."

"You're my best friend, too. Except he was my first."

The two giggled, then clasped a hand over their mouths when they realized the disturbance they were making.

"You must come to our home next week. We can catch up. Let's plan for next Sunday."

Rebecca agreed. When she turned back to Jackson, Hannah's husband, Max Ward, was standing alongside of him, promising to bring in his ranch hands to help Wichita Falls run the auctioneer's off. "More than likely they will have a team of no-gooders along to foil anyone from saving the girls. We will be prepared," Max told the crowd to the agreement of everyone in the room.

Rebecca loved this town, how everyone banded together to save strangers they didn't know. It was going to be a great life, far away from her start in an orphanage, with a man who made her smile so bright. The one who had her heart.

The friends were abundant here.

Families were growing.

Wichita Falls was a good place.

Bad men like John Abbott were not welcome. She hoped he was leading the auction so she could watch as he was driven from their town. He deserved what was coming to him. These men of Wichita Falls wouldn't put up with anyone dirtying up their town.

Except a tiny minuscule of fear reared its ugly head telling Rebecca John Abbott would not go lightly.

The meeting adjourned for the night. The two ladies said their goodbyes, promising to meet up soon.

Jackson held her hand on their walk back to the tiny cabin he was given as part of his job as Sheriff. Rebecca squealed with delight at the pretty yellow daffodils spreading their way across the front walkway. She bent over to pick one and coyly placed it in her hair. Looking up at Jackson, she smiled, her eyes wide and hopeful.

Instead of smiling back, the look in her husband's eyes told her a different story. He lifted her up and with a booted foot, kicked open the door to carry her over the threshold once again.

A giggle erupted from somewhere deep in her throat. Being married to this Sheriff was going to be quite a journey.

<> <>

"The plan is simple. We wait until the auction is set up and the girls are brought out from the wagons. Once every single woman is in our sight, the men in the front two rows will move them out of danger at the count of three so keep yourself alert at all times. Max's men will come in from behind and run them out of town. Everyone clear on their position?"

The men nodded. One farmer, who had stopped at the saloon before gathering in the square, brought up a valid point. "What will we do if they bring one lady out at a time. Saw that in Californy a few years back."

Jackson was prepared for anything. "Then we switch gears. Max has a bag full of money to pay for the women. We don't want to encourage that to be done but we have to make sure the women are not harmed. I don't think it will take much for the auctioneer to have any one of the women put to their death if they figure out we are trying to rescue them. If we can't get them away safely the first time, we pay their price."

"They'll keep on doing such sinful things like this. How will that save other women."

Jackson grinned. "We don't plan to let them off so lightly. Max Ward has some friends in high places. They will be interested in putting these men behind bars. For right now, Max's men will come from behind and get them no matter which way it goes. Be prepared for anything. Keep your head down and the women in safe quarters."

As the crowd dispersed, three covered wagons rolled down the street, kicking up dust as the overworked horses came to a halt in front of the saloon. Two men jumped from the front covered wagon, carrying a hammer, nails and some papers. They began to post flyers on the front of the saloon and several other businesses in the general area.

"Fine people of Wichita Falls, you are all invited to attend our auction in two hours. We'll be set up right here in front of the saloon. Come one, come all at high noon!"

Jackson stood watching from across the street as one of Max's men pretended to stumble from the saloon. "What yer selling, mister?" he asked, slurring his voice.

"You can read, can't you?

The man nodded. "I sure can but my eyesight's a bit dazed today."

"Fine women is what we are auctioning today. You come back at noon then. Bring your friends."

"Let me take a peek at what ya got in them wagons. Then I can tell my friends. I got an awful lot of friends who like to spend their wads."

The husky built man slid from the front of the first wagon. "Alright. You can take a peek. Don't dally too long." His burly hand slid open the back of the covered wagon so the man from the saloon could stick his head inside.

"No talking to them!" His voice boomed. As Jackson watched, he heard voices and mumbling before the man was physically pulled back from the opening. "Go on now! Don't be greedy! Bring your friends. We got eight of 'em here! Another seven in the next wagon. In the last is a feisty creature, she'll be our main attraction."

The man from the saloon sauntered across the street straight towards Sheriff Jackson as the man from the first wagon went inside. Jackson noticed two guards standing firm on each side of the covered wagons. As he guessed, there was no slipping in to rescue the ladies before the auction.

"Jackson, that's him! John Abbott!" His wife waved her arms back and forth, trying to get his attention. She was at the Land Office, far enough away from the saloon so no one would notice her. Jackson had to make sure Abbott didn't see her. He didn't want the Auctioneer to get spooked and high-tail it out of town before they could rescue those poor, distressed women.

He directed her to go inside and began to walk towards the Land Office as if he were taking a stroll. The armed guards at the covered wagons watched him warily since he was the sheriff. Jackson stared back at the men hard. He wasn't about to show them any fear.

He opened the door and entered the Land Office, sliding in between the twenty or so men who hid inside, waiting for his direction. "Thanks for letting us use your office, Dawson."

"Let's get this over with," Dawson told him. He sat at his desk by the window, running a hand through his hair. "I'm not taking a liking to any kinds of trouble these days. Let's run these varmints out of town."

"Here, here!" another one said.

Sheriff Jackson held up his hand. "Listen up, folks. These men will not hesitate to pull the trigger. Those guards are not playing around. They will try to kill you. Let's make sure all the women and children are tucked inside their homes. I need three men to go from business to business and order the ladies and children off the street. Troy, Luke and Bob, the three of you take the main street. Coy, Mack and Robbie, get on over to the mill and make sure the wagon is ready to start rolling out of town at five minutes until noon. We'll use that as a cover."

He turned to Rebecca. "You stay here inside this building. Don't leave under any circumstances. If he see's you, there may be even more trouble. Promise me," Jackson said, his voice stern and yet filled with all the love he had for her.

She ran a hand across his cheek. "I promise."

Jackson walked out the door of the Land Office, wanting to look back because he knew she was peeking out the corner of the window. He didn't dare because he knew the guard's eyes were on him. They wouldn't hesitate to take out the sheriff first. He was the law and order here, no judge to keep them in jail. Not until they could go fetch one. It was primarily a land where men like these roamed wherever they chose to stir up animosity and harm. They thought they were beyond the law of the land.

Not in his town.

Jackson put the badge on to protect this town. His desire to find a place he could call home stirred him beyond the simple duties of a sheriff. He yearned for the simplicity of a small town that was free from sinister acts of violence. As sheriff, he planned to keep Wichita Falls safe.

If it was on his last breath, he would do so.

<> <>

They were all in place. A crowd of men gathered in front of the first wagon. Jackson stood leaning against the wall of the saloon, close enough and yet out of the way of the auctioneer.

The clock struck exactly at noon while the crowd became somewhat larger. Each man hid a handgun in his pant leg or behind him in the waistband of their britches. His deputy was at the front of the crowd incognito to guide the others. Some of the men were getting a bit too excited. Jackson had to place his deputy there to make sure everyone followed direction.

The husky man who had been in charge earlier strolled from the saloon. "Let's get this started! John Abbott, auctioneer at your service. Is everyone ready to see our fine ladies for sale?" At the crowds jeers and nods, he ordered instructions to the guards. "Bring them out!"

Each guard opened the back of the two wagons, lining up the women, forcing each one to stand in a line in front of the crowd. Abbott stood out in the middle of the street, waving towards the women. "These ladies go first, then we'll show you our feature of the day. The one in the third wagon is worth a fortune in gold!"

Jackson swore under his breath. He didn't want to leave one behind before running this ragged, motley crew out of town. All of these ladies were important to someone. Turning towards the deputy, he shook his head slightly so no one would notice.

He had to see how this played out.

"Bring 'em all out, auctioneer! We wanna seem all of 'em before we spend a dime here."

Jackson noticed the wary look in Abbott's eye. They began to dart back and forth as if looking for anything suspicious. Just then a cloud of dust rolled in from outside of town. Jackson knew it was Ward's ranch men coming in too fast. He had to act now. He gave the signal for the men in the front of the crowd to secure the women behind them. As quick as lightening struck, the men in the front row pounced upon the ladies, pushing them further into the crowd.

"What in tar-nation is going on here!" Abbott roared. As a crowd of men on horses blocked one path from town, the auctioneer knew he was in trouble. His armed guards scattered, running in between houses and disappearing from site. Jackson knew it wouldn't take much to round them up but he'd wait on Ward's small army for that. He wanted Abbott.

Abbott was quick for a heavy set man. He jumped up on the last wagon, hollering at the horses to move. The others were keeping the ladies secure, but Jackson knew there was one more in that wagon and it was his duty to save her.

"Oh, my Lands!"

Was that his wife's voice?

Fear crept in to every crevice in his body. He began to run alongside the wagon until it came to a dead stop. He knew the moment Abbott jumped from the wagon. Jackson pulled both pistols from his gun belt, raising them up. The wagon was in his way and the moment Jackson cleared it he stopped dead in his tracks.

"Put the guns down, Sheriff."

He held them out in front of him, staring at his wife, holding a small child in her arms. Horror etched across her face. The little child began to sob. Abbott held a gun to his wife's head.

He closed his eyes. Blinking, he opened them to make sure he wasn't dreaming. If he took a shot at Abbott, which is what he wanted to do, she may well die. Or the child.

"I'm sorry, Jackson. The child. She was in the street. I couldn't do nothing, not with that wagon coming down on her. I was alone. Everyone was gone, I'm so sorry."

Jackson tried hard not to choke on his own words. Stay calm, he reminded himself. You've been through worse.

"I won't say it again, Sheriff. Stand back."

"Let the child go," he warned, his pistols steady.

"Why not. I don't need the kid. Go on."

His wife released the little girl to run screaming down the street. He made sure she was out of harms way before watching in dread as Abbott backed the two of them towards the wagon. "If you try anything, she dies. Plain and simple."

"Then you die, too."

"To be honest, I don't rightly care. But, this one, she owes me."

"Not any more, she is my wife."

The man laughed out loud even if his eyes didn't show it. "Then you owe me and I'll take her without any problems from you."

Desperate and not wanting to show it, Jackson remarked, his voice steady, "Not a chance. There are guns everywhere, Abbott. Give up now."

He barely got the words out before the blunt end of a rifle passed over him like a shadow. He knew he was hit right before darkness took over as he heard his wife's blood curling scream.

Chapter 7

Rebecca watched in horror as her husband was knocked to the ground. One of Abbott's guards had been hiding in an alley between two buildings. Before she had a chance to warn him, he came up behind Jackson. The man cracked a rifle over his head, the sound so loud it made her ears hurt. Please God, please let him live!

She was shoved on the bench as the wagon raced out of town as fast as it could go. The opposite end of town was not guarded as well as the other end, since most of Ward's ranch hands came by the way of the railroad station.

The far end of town had some townsfolk hiding in a wagon filled with bales of hay to surprise anyone trying to slip by. Except when they saw the sheriff's wife on the bench being taken away, they didn't try to rescue her in case she came to harm.

Frustrated, Rebecca stared hard at the small crowd as the horse and wagon galloped past.

"What the tarnations is going on out there! Slow this wagon down, you raving freak!"

A women's voice bellowed from the covered wagon. Abbott laughed. "Shut up back there!"

The guard spoke up, his voice urgent. "Want me to quiet her down, boss? You know, like we did the others."

Abbott took the whip from the side of the wagon and struck it across the guards front. "Don't touch her. She's genuine, prime material and if you as much as lay a hand on her, I will kill you. Understand?"

"Understood, boss."

Abbott looked down at Rebecca. "Can't say as much for you any more since you went and got yourself married. Even so, I can sell you to the men at Mill's Ridge every single night. Or, mayhaps I'll save ya for myself."

"What's Mill's Ridge?" she asked, finally able to find her voice.

"A scathing place of fire and brimstone!" The lady from the back of the wagon's voice rent through the air. "Don't let him fool you! These evil-doers have no heart. At least Abbott won't when I cut it out of his cold, dead body!"

"Don't listen to that woman. She's the one who is evil but she'll fetch me a high dollar. Pure women do bring in so much more. There's someone out there who will buy her in a heartbeat. I thought I'd find that at that little town of yours, Wichita Falls. Except all I found was trouble and you."

"We gonna go back and get those other girls, boss?"

Abbott chewed on his bottom lip. "Ain't no use now, not with everyone trying to bring ill repute upon us. I'll have to up the ante and find me some more of those mail order fools."

Rebecca seethed. Unable to keep quiet any longer, she struck out in the only way she knew, with words. "You will be hunted down like a dog, Mr. Abbott! When Jackson wakes up, he'll go to the ends of the earth to find you."

"Ain't no mister there, girlie. He's a hood-swindling dog, just like you says. Tell 'em sister!"

The guards voice mumbled something Rebecca wasn't able to make out, but the girl laughed again, her voice shrill. "You ain't gonna do nothing to me, I'm too valuable, just ask your boss!"

Abbott laughed out loud. "Right you are, and a fiery one at that. Now shut your lips and let me get this wagon back to Mill's Ridge. As for you, maybe your husband will never wake up. That knock on the head may have done him in."

His horrible words caused her to be quiet. She rode in silence the rest of the way. Jackson had to be alive! If he were not, she would feel it in her heart. Looking up, she begged God for her husband's safety so that he may come for her. It was the only hope she had.

They entered a town much like Wichita Falls except it was dirty and unkempt. Houses looked abandoned, some had windows covered up with wood and nails. The saloon was lively, it seemed to be one of the few places in town that had any life. The wagon slowed to a stop in front of the saloon. Abbott got down and headed for the doors. He threw an order to his guard. "Take those two to the shanty and don't let either one out of your site."

The guard held the arm of each girl. Rebecca tried to push her hair aside but was held so tightly she didn't get a good look at the other prisoner until they were locked into a small adobe room with a chair and a bed. The dirt floor smelled musty, almost causing her to gag.

"You'll get used to the smell. After awhile, it won't bother you at all."

Rebecca stared at the beautiful redhead with long, thick wavy hair that rolled down her back like the sparkling flowing waterfall in Wichita Falls. She wore a long magenta colored gown with puffy half sleeves and cut so low the white skin of her bosom showed. "I see why John Abbott called you red. You have beautiful hair."

The girl grunted. "Thank you, kindly, but it does me no good out here stuck in this God-forsaken place. Now that you are here, we have to escape. I can see you are a strong willed woman, unlike the other ladies who whimpered and cried day and night. I wanted to slap them silly with all their nonsense. Acting like a bunch of babies, there was no talking any sense at all. They were doomed, they kept saying, driving me to squeeze the palms of my hands over my ears so I didn't hear them any more."

"I'm certain they were terrified. My name is Rebecca."

The fiery redhead held out her dirt stained hand. "Sophia Jordon at your service. This here is Mill's Ridge, the worst town you will ever be in. It consists of outlaws, hooligans and lazy no good rotten men and even some awful women."

"How did you get here, Sophia?"

Rebecca sat on the wooden bench beside her. She may as well get as comfortable as possible. It looked like they would be here awhile. At least until Jackson came to her rescue. A trace of fear entered her heart. What if he was hurt so badly, he was not able to come for her.

A shiver went down Rebecca's spine so fast it felt as if a butterfly was scraping its wings from her neck to her waist. She didn't dare wait to see if someone was going to rescue her. This woman was right. They had to escape.

"Please, call me Sophie, nothing fancy about me at all. Sophia is for ladies and I sure ain't no lady, not any more."

Rebecca frowned. "Don't be absurd. You certainly look like a lady to me."

Sophie smiled. "Thank you. It's been hard being in this prison for so long. We took Mamma to Dallas to see if the doctors there could help her sickness, but she died soon after. Me and Daddy came back to the cabin to farm the land right outside of this town. A few years back it was filled with people like us, hard-working folks, but then the bad men came along." Her voice broke but Rebecca didn't know her well enough to give any type of comfort. So she sat and waited for Sophie to get a hold of herself.

"They killed my father and forced me to rot in this room. They are trying to sell me because I am pure, but they haven't found anyone with enough money to buy me. The men in this town are all no-good, broke and worthless sonsofguns. They need the money my so called purity will bring. These men are all evil and I hope God strikes each and every man down."

"I'm so sorry, Sophie. Where are the rest of the townsfolk?"

"Gone. Most ran away, some went back to Dallas, a few families fled to Wichita Falls. We are dead set in the middle between the two. Once there was a wonderful man passing through who tried to help us but he was driven from the town. Then, on his way out, he saved a family from being beaten by killing the man who tried to do them harm. The outlaws here put a price on his head and no one has seen him since. Until today."

Rebecca perked up. "Today? What do you mean?"

"That mighty handsome Sheriff saved the Sellingsgrove family from certain death before he had to flee the town. If he comes back here, he'll be strung up like a spring chicken. There's bad men here. Men that will do him ill will if he returns."

Rebecca doubled over, hugging her stomach. Taking in a deep breath, unhealthy shivers riveted through her whole body. She sniffed, sick already from the musty, cellar-like room. "He will return."

Sophie shrugged. "I hope not. I'd hate to see such a handsome man killed. We have to get out of here. I've been thinking about this for a long time. There is a way out but we'll have to wait until tonight. I may even be able to get us some food and water and a horse to take us to Wichita Falls. Is that where you want to go? I just want away from this sprawling hole in the wall town."

Rebecca placed two shaking hands over her face. "Oh, please, no! Say it isn't so!" The desperation in her voice caused Sophie to look concerned.

"Rebecca, what is it? I thought you were tough, like me? Now you are snivelling like those other women did."

"It's not that. The sheriff is my husband. He will come here for me, that's a fact."

Sophie froze. "Oh, no! Then we better not wait for dark. We have to put our plan in motion now."

<><>

"That was too easy, Sophie. How long do you think it will be before they notice the room is empty?"

Sophie was huffing and puffing, trying to catch her breath. The two ladies had set up a plan to distract the guard. "They won't even notice, not for a few more hours. By then, we should be in Wichita Falls. The sun is starting to go down, so we must hurry. Giddy-up." Sophie was riding astride the horse, her legs sticking out from her dress. She showed Rebecca how to get on behind her and they took off like a bat escaping from its cave. Since the town was nearly empty and everyone was occupied in the saloon, no one noticed their disappearance.

When they were clear of Mill's Ridge, Rebecca giggled. "I must say, I can't believe we did that."

Sophie laughed with her. "When you picked up the chamberpot and threw the contents in his face, I thought surely we were doomed. It wasn't enough to stop him, but then when you knocked him on the head with the chamberpot and he slumped to the ground, I knew it was our chance to go, even without provisions. He never had a chance to call for help. Thanks be to

God above. But we have to hurry, it'll be dark soon and we don't know our way back too well."

It was well past dark by the time the two women made their way down main street in Wichita Falls, exhausted from the long ride. Rebecca knew the handkerchief she used to stuff in the guards mouth wouldn't keep him down for long, or the make-shift cloth around his hands, but it was the best they could find in the room. She prayed those horrible men wouldn't come back here to try to hurt anyone.

Was she going to put this wonderful little town at risk by her presence alone? Should she even be here with a man like John Abbott on the loose? Had it been a mistake to marry her best friend knowing Abbott could come here at any time now and her husband was placed in harm's way?

Rebecca slid from the horse, running to the Sheriff's office. It was dark. She ran across the street, hoping the Land Office was still open, that someone would be there but found it also dark. The door was locked. Making her way to the back of the building where Dawson and Grace lived in the house behind the office, she banged on the door. A small light shone in the window. Grace hurried to the door, peeking out before her eyes widened in shock at seeing Rebecca and Sophie standing there.

The door was thrown open. "Rebecca! Come in. How in the world did you get here? Oh no! Oh no! The men! They went after you!"

Rebecca froze. "To Mill's Ridge?" She stumbled through the kitchen to sit on the chair Grace pulled out for her.

"Yes. The Sheriff was in the lead. Almost every man in this town went with him to Mill's Ridge knowing it was occupied with outlaws and horrible men. This town is standing united. They will not allow bad men to do anyone harm."

Rebecca felt sick. Her new friend Sophie placed an arm around her shoulder. "It will be okay. Most of the men will be too drunk by now to stand up to anyone, let alone a whole band of men. They are all cowards, only fierce and mean when they are in a group. By now, there will be a small handful in the saloon, most of the others passed out."

"But, they are deadly, they can draw a gun and hurt someone from this town. Oh, God, please keep our men safe!" Rebecca clutched her stomach again, sick now, afraid someone would be terribly hurt through all of this.

Grace turned to Sophie. "You must be the lady in the last wagon, the one these men were trying to sell as a prize. My name is Grace, pleased to meet you."

Sophie nodded. "I'm Sophie. Can we get cleaned up here? Would you mind?"

Grace gasped. "How rude of me. Yes, let's get you two cleaned up and out of those awful, dirty clothes. I have something that will fit you for now. The other women can help. Ruby! Lily! Hannah! Charity!"

Four women rushed from the other room, curious to see what was going on. After a lengthy explanation, all of the women got busy. Ruby and Charity began to make some tea and warm up broth for the ladies. Lilly and Hannah got some warm water ready for the ladies to clean up. For over two hours, the ladies took care of business.

All of them were sitting around the dark, pine table having tea when Miss Addie tapped on the glass then burst through the door.

"Why isn't that door locked?"

Grace smiled. "It was, up until about two hours ago. Miss Addie, this is Sophie, she helped to rescue our Rebecca."

Rebecca let those words flow all around her. She was welcomed here in this town with open arms. No longer an orphan, the ugly past was always something she never quite got over, until now. Tonight, she felt as if she belonged to a group of people who loved her.

The others listened as Sophie told her story. Rebecca kept watching the door in hopes her husband would walk through but after a few hours, he never did.

Fear rose up. It was so simple a task and obviously her husband was trained for this. After all, he had put on that badge. All he had to do was go in and clear out the varmints in that awful town. "Shouldn't they be back by now?" Rebecca asked the one question no one else was wanting to speak up about.

Miss Addie tried to keep up everyone's spirits. "It may be they had to stay put, wait for daylight before heading back. I can't rightly send any man out there this time of night. It's too dark and dangerous."

That was what Rebecca was afraid of.

"Perhaps you should try to get a few hours sleep. I can clearly see you're exhausted." Miss Addie's concerned voice was like honey to a swarm of bees.

"I can't possibly close my eyes. Not until I know Jackson is alive and well."

"I don't think you have to worry. That knock on the head didn't keep him down for long. He was up and stirring up a posse not long afterwards. We are proud to have him as our sheriff."

Rebecca let a tear slip down her cheek. "I'm proud to have him as my husband." She looked up to the ceiling. "Please, God, keep him safe."

"Amen." The others followed suit, taking the hand of the one sitting next to them, starting a prayer chain around the oblong table. The oil lamp flickered through the room, providing a glow for the women as they prayed for the safety and return of their men.

Chapter 8

Jackson stood at the edge of town, his memory filled with the last time he entered this God-forsaken town. The place looked deserted, even though he knew halfway through town there was a saloon that stayed open most of the night. It was in that place the rotten men who feared no man were occupied with booze and ill-fated talk.

The posse was ready. They had ridden hell bent for leather until the horses needed to rest to get here in one piece. Jackson scanned the buildings. Where was she? Fear for his wife rose up from within. He had never asked God for a darn thing but tonight he raised his head to the clouds.

"I may not be worthy of you, but I ask for the safety of the woman I love." He didn't care who heard him. Rebecca had become his life. If he had to openly pray for her, he didn't give a darn who heard.

But the tiny mumbles behind him gave courage and strength to his weary body and mind. "Amen," he heard clear as a bell, muttered in monotones and in panicked men's voices.

He was a leader. His role as sheriff made him so. He looked behind and beside him. The men who had claimed Wichita Falls as their own stood beside him, ready to help rescue his wife.

It was a matter of principle in Wichita Falls. The men were filled with obligation and duty, full of love, honor and respect for their neighbor. He turned in his saddle. "I'm proud of every man here tonight. Thank you for bearing this with me."

He felt a strong hand on his shoulder. Marshall Montgomery nodded. "We're in this together, Sheriff. Now let's get this done."

There were so many men who rode with him tonight, it almost had Jackson smiling. He was so proud of them. Marshall had brought in five of his best ranch hands, including Maximilian, an older gentleman who was quick with a gun. There were stories of Mac riding with a famous gang that was not talked about in Wichita Falls. No one knew for sure if it was true because it had happened when he was a young man.

Dawson and Ben Sloan rode beside him, ready to help. Dawson owned the Land Office and his brother owned the only hotel in Wichita Falls. They didn't hesitate to saddle up when the Sheriff needed help.

Max Ward, the richest ranch man in the whole territory had twenty five men in his wake. They were all spread in various places around Mill's Ridge, ready to jump in at the first signal. The cowboys were brave and fearless.

Daniel hung back, wanting to take it all in as he was the owner of the only newspaper in the region. He was no lightweight though, and would assist as necessary.

"Well, then, are you ready?" Marshall Montgomery urged.

Sheriff nodded. "I don't want my wife harmed. I will give my life before there is a hair on her body damaged. Do you all understand? No matter what, she leaves here in one piece."

The others nodded, even though he couldn't see them in the darkness. But he knew, if it came down to it, his life was not as important as his beloved wife. It was clear now and going into battle would be easier knowing all these men understood.

"Let's take them by surprise!"

<> <>

One man was left at the bar, his back to Jackson. The others put up a good fight, but most were on the ground, hurt or dead.

Some tried to flee in to the night to no avail. Every single man was stopped. It took less than fifteen minutes.

Except for the one man in front of him Jackson wanted to put a slug through his heart for kidnapping his wife. "Where is she?"

"Gone."

Ripples of dread ran down his spine. "Gone where? What did you do with my wife?" Jackson took a step closer to him. He had to be careful, with the man's back to him, he could be holding a weapon that Jackson couldn't see.

"How should I know! I'm not going to tell you where she is! Do you think I am an idiot?" John Abbott's slurred voice got under his skin. He wanted to hurt him, bad. He had to keep his cool. Drunken men were dangerous.

Taking another step towards the bar, Jackson pulled the hammer back. The sound of the click made it obvious he would shoot if Abbott made the wrong move. "Where is my wife?

The man shrugged. "Ask Willy. He's the dumb jerk who let them overtake him. I left him back in the sod house across the street, stuffed his mouth shut after he told me they escaped. Idiot let two women lock him in there."

Hope escalated. Jackson almost smiled at the thought of his wife escaping from here. "That's twice now she foiled you. Don't you think by now, Abbott, there is no escaping the consequences of your actions? I should let you hang on the tree outside this saloon the moment the sun comes up. Instead, I am going to watch you rot in a jail and when you're trial comes up, I'll be there to watch you hang by the hands of justice served."

"I won't be foiled again." For an oversized man, he moved quickly. Jackson was ready for him. He pumped the trigger, watching as the man jerked from the impact of the bullet hitting his chest. But right before he slid to the ground, the knife in his hand came flying towards Jackson. Too late, it hit him in the shoulder, causing blood to squirt and soil his shirt.

Jackson was knocked back a bit. He stumbled before reaching up and pulling the blade from the flesh. Blood gushed even more. He held the palm of his hand over the wound as he strolled to the body on the ground. Jackson wanted to make sure the man was dead.

He stared at the man who had abducted his wife. Anger so strong pushed him to pull the hammer back again. He wanted to empty his gun in the man's gut.

"He's dead." Marshall Montgomery fell in beside him. "No use wasting a bullet. Let's get that wound looked at."

Jackson slowly let the trigger back. He was glad Montgomery showed up just now. "Guess you're right. But not here, we need to search this place and see where my wife is hiding out. I'm sure she didn't leave in the thick of night, not with it so dark outside." Even as he said the words, he figured that was exactly what she did. Who would want to stick around a horrible place like this?

Most of the men gathered in the street. A smell so pungent permeated through the air. Men coughed and spit, gagging at the retched odor. "Found this man tied up in that little shod house over yonder," one of the ranch hands offered.

Jackson recognized the stinky man as one of the guards from the wagon in Wichita Falls. Even though it was hard to stand next to him, he walked over and yanked the cloth from the man's mouth.

A yelp so loud and painful came from his throat. He wailed into the night like a wounded bear.

"Shut yer mouth, stinkpot!" Someone from the crowd hollered.

The rest of the men began to laugh at the pathetic excuse of a man standing in their midst. "That's enough!" Jackson ordered. "Each man has their own story. This here one, I'm not sure but from the looks of things, he met a chamberpot head on."

The man cringed. "Those two women came at me like wild cats from the jungles of the Amazon! I didn't stand a chance. By the time I figured out what they were doing, I was knocked out."

Jackson laughed. "You let two dainty women knock you out with a chamberpot?"

"Like I said, they took me by surprise!"

Jackson almost gagged, but got closer to the man. "Where are they? You tell me right now or I'll hand you over to this rowdy crowd."

Cheers went up all around the man. He looked around, fear in his eyes at the multitudes of men surrounding him. "I swear, man, I don't know. The only thing I remember after I came to was the sound of horse's hooves fading in the distance. Figured it was them women bailing out."

Jackson was relieved to know they were smart enough to take a horse. What scared him more than anything was the fact they would be out in the night, without any weapons to protect themselves. He was glad to know she wasn't alone. The woman in the last wagon must be with her. Relief went through him. Jackson swayed a bit at the loss of blood but he wanted to find his wife.

He turned to get on his horse.

A shot rang out.

He felt something whip past his head and knock his hat to the ground. Wetness trailed down his temple, past his chin. He stood swaying back and forth. Guns slid from leather, triggers cocked so fast it was hard to keep the noises straight. Shot after shot rang out from the crowd of men surrounding him.

Jackson stared in silence at the bloody mass that had been the guard. No longer able to focus, everything became a blur. He felt the hard leather of his saddle as it pressed into his back.

"He's going down." The words sounded like they were spoken in slow motion. Jackson didn't care. All he wanted was to see his wife. Her name formed on his lips. "Becky," he whispered. "Becky." Desperation made him hold on.

But gravity and blood loss took him over the edge of reality into a world of dismal dreams.

Rebecca paced back and forth. She was sure by now someone would have rode in with some answers. The last few hours had been way too quiet. Even though she knew better, sleep evaded her. There was no sleeping with Jackson in Mill's Ridge. She turned to the other ladies. "I need some air."

"We'll come with you."

Seven women wrapped shawls around their shoulders and took to the porch of the Land Office. No one stopped them. Addie had been out on the porch already, a rifle slung over her lap. When she saw the other ladies, she smiled. "No sense in just sitting there, waiting and pacing the floor. I'm helping to guard this town."

That was the thing in Wichita Falls. Women, men, even strangers that come upon this small, growing town who decide to stay begin to feel protective of every single person there.

"You've been here a long time, Miss Addie?" Sophie asked, her fingers making a rhythmic sound along the wooden porch rail.

"I've been here since day one," the older woman said softly.

Grace spoke up. "Forgive me for asking, but have you ever been in love?"

Addie shifted in her seat. "Once. A long time ago. I came here as a mail-order bride, you know. I wanted to get far away from my father. He was so mean and had ordered me to marry a man I didn't care for. After doing some research and contacting a matrimonial agency, I picked up and left. I was set to marry this rich farmer who had a big ranch out here. Turned out he was trying to swindle my land certificates that I had inherited from a family member."

"What did you do, Miss Addie?"

She grinned. "This stranger in town warned me not to marry him. Back then Wichita Falls was filled with outlaws and questionable men. But this one man, he informed me what the man was trying to do. Through our letters, I had told him about my certificates and he came up with the idea to have me believe he was rich with a farm beyond the town. I ate it up like a little kitten on warm milk at first."

"How did you know he wanted to swindle you."

"Because he bragged about it in the saloon. If you ever want to know what is going on with anyone in town, just sit in a saloon."

"We can't rightly do that, Miss Addie."

"That's why I listened when this stranger told me how I was going to be swindled. I asked him why he'd care about a girl like me. Then he kissed me and I knew right then and there I'd never marry another soul. No matter what they were trying to do."

"What a romantic story."

"It's not over." Miss Addie sighed, her hand resting on the barrel of the gun as she stared into the night. "I refused to marry the swindler and vowed to never let anyone dupe me again. My handsome stranger became my admirer. He courted me for many months after that. He asked me to marry him. I told him I would think about it."

"You did what? Why, Miss Addie, he sounded as if he was so in love with you."

"I felt deep down there was something he wasn't telling me. Turned out to be right. Ever since the first man tried to swindle me, I have had this knack for feeling a person out. I wasn't wrong even if he was the love of my life."

"Oh, dear, what happened to him?"

"I built my boarding house and became a business woman. I told him if he wanted to marry me, he'd have to accept the fact that I was going to become an independent woman. Back then, this town was wild, too many rowdy men and not enough women. I knew I should marry, but I had already begun to set myself apart as someone who didn't take no sass from any man. I vowed this town would become a town where families could grow and decent men and women would walk the street. They laughed at me back then."

"They're not laughing now," Rebecca spoke aloud.

"No, they are not."

"But what happened to this man you loved?" Charity wondered.

"Two Pinkerton men came to town one day looking for him. Turned out he was an outlaw wanted for some crimes while he rode with a gang. The day they carted him off, I must have cried for two weeks straight. The man had lied. He had me believe he was a decent man, ready to settle down and he was an outlaw trying not to get caught."

Rebecca pondered on her words. "Actually, Miss Addie, and I don't mean no disrespect, but it sounds like he was an outlaw trying to reform himself."

Miss Addie frowned. Regret showered her face, her eyes hauntingly sad. "He spent his time in prison. Paid his dues. When he was relieved from that place, he came back to find me. Wanted to apologize for lying to me. He even asked if we could start over again but it was too late."

"That's a beautiful but sad story, Miss Addie."

"It didn't end well. By then I was helping to build this town. We had decent people here, families were coming every day to start a new life and all the riff-raff were long gone after the railroad was built. People trusted me. I had even began my matchmaking services to bring more decent women here. When he came back to this town, I knew he couldn't stay. He was a confirmed outlaw."

"He did his time. He had to start over somewhere."

"I rebuked him. Perhaps I was a bit too harsh. But I told him in front of God and everyone it would be a cold day in the land of the dead before I would marry a convict."

"Oh, you didn't, Miss Addie. Did you love him still?"

She hung her head. "To this very day. But I had made a promise that I would not go back on."

"What did he do, leave?"

She shook her head. "No, he's still here. I doubt anyone today would know about him anymore. Most of the folks that knew about our relationship are gone or moved on."

"He's here?" Rebecca asked in wonder. "In this town?"

"Not exactly in town. He is close by. Back then, he refused to leave. Told me he would love me forever, even if I hated him. I never told him that I didn't hate him so he took that as I still cared."

"Oh, Miss Addie. Yours is truly a tale of woe. Why don't you just swallow your pride and tell him how you feel?" Rebecca could never keep her love for Jackson to herself.

"Because a promise is a promise. My word is the only thing I have."

The seven women shook their heads in unison. "No, Miss Addie, you have worked with every one of us to bring love in to our lives. All the while, you have been starving yourself of what is truly the most important thing of all. We can't let this happen to you."

Miss Addie shrugged. "Not much you can do, Rebecca. My mind was made up many years ago."

The women all looked at each other. Ideas began to form in Rebecca's head. There had to be a way to change her mind. After all, it was a modern age now, unlike the past where times were a bit more strict. She noticed the others were pondering the same thing and knew right then they would work together to find out who the love of her life was.

"This town isn't that big that we can't find someone." Rebecca didn't realize she spoke out loud.

Heads popped up. "My thoughts exactly," Ruby mentioned. Rebecca smiled at her. They would find out who this man was sooner or later, maybe give Miss Addie some of her own matchmaking services.

A lone rider galloped through town, stirring up dust along the way. From the front porch of the Land Office the saloon sat in full view. The man jumped from his mare and ran into the saloon. Each and every lady on the front porch stood at attention, trying to see what they could.

"Wonder why one rider is back and not the others. Do you see anything out there?"

Heads turned to the edge of town but it was too black to see anything at all. Eight heads whipped back to the saloon when the rider came out with his hands full. He lunged back on the horse and took off like a rabbit leaping from his hole.

The bartender, Salem Nightingale, stood at the door watching the lone rider. He had a mug in one hand and a towel slung over his shoulder.

"What in carnation happened?" Rebecca stood hanging on to the rail, trying to see into the distance.

"Not sure but I aim to find out," Sophia told the others. She was halfway across the street before anyone knew what she was doing.

"Come back here! You can't go in to a saloon," Ruby told her.

Sophie walked backwards, smiling and determined. "Who says I'm going in there. Why, that fine gentleman may be able to answer our questions."

Rebecca and the others watched as the two exchanged words. Salem Nightingale's voice carried in the wind, but it was still too far away to discern. All at once, Sophie put her arms out and curtsied as if he were a gentleman in a parlor hall.

The girls began to giggle as Sophie ran across the street, Salem shouting after her. He leaned up against the wall staring after her, a wide grin on his face. Rebecca could see that clearly.

When Sophie returned to the porch she was fuming and out of breath. "What an intolerable man! To think I was endeared at first at his tall and dark features, let alone his surly deep voice. Well, this girl will never get close to the likes of him again!"

Then Rebecca noticed how Sophie turned to watch Salem staring at her. She curtsied once again from her place on the porch right before the bartender pushed away from the wall and went inside. A few moments later the place went dark.

"Sophie, what did you learn?" Rebecca wrung her hands. There was still no sign of her husband or anyone else except that one lone rider.

"You'll be happy to know most of the men are on there way here. One of the men was in bad shape, so that fellow came to get more supplies. They had to stop a few miles down the road because he was bleeding so bad. Name of Jackson something or other."

Rebecca gripped on to the wooden railing with all her might. "Jackson," she whispered. "My husband was hurt?"

Sophie gasped. "I didn't realize Jackson and the Sheriff were one and the same!" She tried to smooth things over but all Rebecca had heard was her husband was in bad shape. She turned to the others. "I have to get to him. Now."

"It's too dark to go out there, Rebecca. Let's go inside. Have a cup of tea. We will have to wait there."

"No. I can't wait." She looked at each and every one of them. "If that was your husband out there, what would you do?"

Miss Addie stood. "I'll get the buggy." She ran down the street, holding tight onto the rifle while Charity, Ruby and Lily went to help get the buggy.

"I'll stay with the children," Sophie offered.

"So will I," Grace told her. "Between the two of us, we can start making some breakfast. It will be daylight soon and the men will be starving after their night."

Rebecca turned to the others. Tears welled in her eyes. "Thank you," she whispered, unable to speak any louder less she choke on her own words. Devastated to the core, the thought of her husband not making it was torn from her thoughts. She had to go to him.

The buggy pulled to a stop in front of the Land Office.

Salem Nightingale was locking up the saloon. He strolled across the street when he saw the buggy filled with women. "What is going on here this time of night?"

Sophie placed her hands on her hips. "Well, hello to you, Sir Nightingale. Need I curtsey again? Unfortunately, I don't have time. Rebecca is going to Sheriff Montana."

A hurl of cuss words erupted from Salem's mouth. The women ignored him as they planned to persue their original idea.

He looked at Sophie then at the four women inside the open air buggy. "Move on over, ladies." His tall frame jumped up on the driver seat as he took the reins, mumbling as the horse was guided down the street.

Sophie grinned.

Rebecca blew her a kiss. Thank you, she mouthed at her new friend. With Salem driving the buggy, she felt reassured they would get there in one piece with an experienced driver. And quicker than Miss Addie could.

Chapter 9

The buggy rolled to a stop. Jackson tried hard to keep his eyes focused. His whole body felt as if he were in a cloud, floating around the men who surrounded him, dabbing at the blood on his shoulder and head. He saw Salem jump down, then reached out a hand to help Rebecca. She didn't wait for him though, instead took a leap from the buggy as if her life depended on it.

A smile curved at his mouth.

"You think this is funny?" Marshall Montgomery mumbled.

Jackson tried to form her name to let Marshall know why he smiled now. Nothing came out, his mouth was cracked and dry. His head felt as if it were split open from the pounding of horse's hooves that got him this far. It was no fun to be slumped over the saddle immobile while the large animal pounded the dirt. Every single bone and joint ached with a fierceness like no other.

He felt her presence before she was up close, kissing his cheek through the blood that splotched his face. "Oh, my Jackson, be strong. You are my best friend. My love."

Her soft hands cupped his face. Soft lips touched his own hard, dry ones. He felt himself drifting off again, the air around him fading while he floated on thick blades of grass. *I love you*, he told her even if no words came out.

She continued to cling to him. He felt her softness, even as he was lifted in to the buggy. She placed herself by his side, her hands caressing his skin, sliding up and down his arm. The burning sensation from the wound on his shoulder lightened. He focused on her worried face, couldn't peel his eyes from her beautiful skin.

"I love you," he was able to croak out at last. She stirred beside him, running her finger along his jaw. "As I love you, Jackson. Always. Forever. Don't leave me, I beg of you."

He tried to lift a hand to touch her. His head banged like a warrior's drum when he tried to shake it back and forth so he stilled. Closing heavy lids, it was okay now to sleep. His love was here. She would care for him. "Sleep, darling," she whispered. "Take care. Go to sleep."

So, he did.

<><>

Jackson was in his bed. He knew it before he tried to open his eyes. He didn't want to get up. Funny, his shoulder no longer hurt, his head felt fine. No banging kept him awake at night any more. He knew he had been in and out of consciousness for awhile. Even if he had no idea of how long. Was it hours or days?

With a bold movement, he sat straight up to find himself alone in an empty room.

Where was she? "Becky?" he croaked, his voice still raspy.

Movement from the other side of the door stirred his curiosity. He stumbled from the blankets, cautious to stand for a moment until the dizziness passed. His legs were wobbly as if he hadn't been using them in a long time. He reached out to place a hand on the wall to keep him steady. With focused steps, Jackson made his way to the door, turning the knob to find his wife pushing a rocking chair from one end of the room to the other.

"Hi," he told her, before she looked up and screamed!

"Jackson!" she whispered as if she had seen a ghost.

He pushed off the wall, taking a few steps to her side. She reached out to him, placing her arms around his waist. "Let's get you to the chair." She turned the rocker towards him and helped him to sit.

"It feels as if I haven't used my legs in months."

Rebecca turned her head at a slight angle. She had tears dripping from her face. Getting on her knees, she placed her head in his lap, her shoulders shaking like he'd never seen before. It seemed like just yesterday when he felt her touch as he was lifted in to the buggy.

The wetness from her tears seeped on to his shirt. "Hey now, settle down, Becky. I'm fine. I could use a glass of water."

She struggled to her feet and quickly poured him a glass. As he drank, she touched his face, tears still streaming down as she touched every part of him as if he were indeed a ghost. "Becky, why the tears? I'm fine, really."

Becky curled on to his lap, her face in his shoulder. She breathed in his scent and began to cry again. He held her, not understanding her strange behavior. Had something happened to her? Was she touched now that she had gone through all of this with John Abbott? Was his wife's mind too far gone?

After several minutes, Jackson nudged her to look at him. "Becky, what is it? What's wrong?"

She took a shattering deep breath. "You were gone, Jackson. Your brain was not working."

He laughed. "What do you mean my brain was not working?"

"Your body was in such a deep state of sleep, when you didn't wake up after a few days, we called for the doctor in Dallas. We were too afraid to move you. He came and told us you were brain dead, like a vegetable in the garden. No movement, nothing would wake you. He said that you would be like this forever. That I should prepare for the worst."

Jackson wiped the flowing tears from her face. "I'm not brain dead. As you can see, I'm fine. Except for feeling a bit weak and tired, my mind is the same as its always been."

"We didn't know. You were so still. I stayed by your side every single day, reading to you, talking, praying for you to wake up. God is good. The whole town has been praying for you and he answered our prayers."

"I'm sorry you had to deal with this, Becky. I love you."

"I love you right back, Jackson Montana."

Jackson pushed back on the chair, rocking the two of them. "I didn't know we had a rocking chair."

"We didn't. I just received this from Sears. I had ordered it a few weeks ago."

"Thank you. It makes this room look nice. Much nicer than the old chairs I had."

"Well, there's a reason for everything, you know that, right?"

He was still a bit foggy but felt as if she were trying to tell him something. "Yes, most of the time there is a reason for every single thing under God's green planet."

"Jackson?"

"Hmm," he murmured, liking the feel of his wife curled in his arms. He closed his eyes, taking in her lavender scent.

"When you were ten years old, did you ever think about having a family?"

"Not really. Not until I was older. I hated being an only child, an orphan. When you came along, it was like I had my own sister to hang out with. Except we weren't sister and brother, of course."

"What if I told you we have the chance to make our own family."

He opened his eyes. "What are you saying, Becky? Are you with child?"

She nodded, tears pooling in her eyes now. The realization of what she had been dealing with, not knowing if he would ever come out of his stupor hit Jackson full force. "Oh Becky, darling." He held her in his arms for so long it began to get dark in the room.

She reached up and took his hand, gently laying it across her stomach. "We're going to be parents," she whispered. "It's still hard to believe."

He left his hand there, in wonder, waiting to feel a tiny beat of this little life they created. It didn't come but he knew in that moment that there would be many little hearts beating right where he placed his hand.

"We'll need a bigger house."

"Can we afford one on a sheriff's salary?" she teased.

"What we need is a farm, not a house in town. It will be big enough to raise our own children and maybe a child or two from an orphanage."

"Truly?"

When Jackson nodded, he was surprised to hear Becky had the same dream. "Let it be a child no one wants. Someone we can take in and give them all of our love."

Jackson drew her in, touching his mouth to hers. "I'll work two jobs if I have to, my love. We'll find a way to provide a big enough home for our own kids as well as other lost orphans."

"I think I saw just the place the other day. There's an abandoned two story house about a mile from town. A family from the city bought it but then left so quickly they even left furniture behind. Sold it to the land office within a week of buying the place. It's close enough for you to get to your job as sheriff and far enough from town where we can have chickens and maybe some horses and, oh, the possibilities!" Rebecca's stomach tightened. Jackson thought he felt a tiny kick.

"Was that the baby?" he asked in awe.

"I think it's too soon, but you never know."

"My son will be very astute. He may be agreeing with us."

Rebecca laughed. "How do you know she isn't agreeing with us?"

Jackson kissed her. "How do we know there isn't one of each?"

Her eyes grew as big as the saucer underneath the cup of tea sitting on the edge of the table. "That would be absolutely wonderful but I'm not sure my body can manage two at one time."

"After what we've been through, our God can help us manage anything. Anything at all."

"I love you, Jackson Montana."

"I love you too, Rebecca Montana. I'm glad you let me sit with you under that library window so long ago."

She smiled at him, her heart filled with love and joy. "I think we were meant to be."

"It's been so long since I've held you in my arms, darling. Let's go to bed."

Rebecca laughed. "I've been in your arms every single night."

"Yes, but I was brain dead, remember? I never knew. I have a lot of making up to do."

"You sure do, husband."

<> <>

Thank you for reading Rebecca and Jackson's story. As always, if it weren't for my readers, these stories wouldn't continue. I wonder if Sophie will continue on her trek to find a husband? Her first journey as a mail order bride was delayed when John Abbott got in the way. Will Miss Addie complete her wish to send Sophie on her way now that all the girls agreed to let Miss Addie find them a husband? Or, will Salem Nightingale get in Sophie's way?

Get your copy of Sophie on Amazon Available NOW![1] (https://www.amazon.com/Sophie-Order-Brides-Wichita-Falls-ebook/dp/B06XX6XRQ5/ ref=sr_1_sc_1?ie=UTF8&qid=1491228459&sr=8-1-spell&keywords=sophie+mail+order+bridesof+wichita+falls)

---

1. https://www.amazon.com/Sophie-Order-Brides-Wichita-Falls-ebook/dp/B06XX6XRQ5/ref=sr_1_sc_1?ie=UTF8&qid=1491228459&sr=8-1-spell&keywords=sophie+mail+order+bridesof+wichita+falls

OR

Do you like to read the whole box set in one shot.

Volume 1 Books 1-8 Ebooks

Available now on Amazon[2]

(https://www.amazon.com/gp/product/B076YXYBN8)

---

2. https://www.amazon.com/gp/product/B076YXYBN8

Books by Cyndi Raye

Mail Order Brides of Wichita Falls Series

Ruby

Grace

Lily

Charity

Hannah

Rebecca

Sophie

Ellie

Jenna

Leila

Boxed Set Vol 1

Boxed Set Vol 2

Christmas in Wichita Falls Holiday Book

Brides of Mill Ridge Series

An Outlaws Honor

A Reverend's Rose

The Ranger's Redemption

A Doctor's Devotion

A Teacher's Treasure

A Sister's Sanctuary

Sons of Nora White Series

A Bride for Luke

A Bride for Adam

A Bride for Samuel

A Groom for Nora

A Bride for Russell

A Bride for Wesley

A Groom for Widow Young

Multi-Author Series Contributions

A Bride for Abel - The Proxy Brides Book #4

A Bride for Calvin - The Proxy Brides

A Bride for Arthur - The Proxy Brides

An Agent for Carolina - The Pinkerton Matchmaker

An Agent for Cari - The Pinkerton Matchmaker

A Tin Star for Christmas - The Belles of Wyoming

Stealing My Heart - The Belles of Wyoming

Candy Cane Christmas - Ornamental Matchmaker Book #10

All these books and more new releases can be found by visiting
https://www.amazon.com/Cyndi-Raye/e/B00ENA1WEG

Don't miss out!

Visit the website below and you can sign up to receive emails whenever Cyndi Raye publishes a new book. There's no charge and no obligation.

https://books2read.com/r/B-A-PXQ-FIMFC

BOOKS 2 READ

Connecting independent readers to independent writers.